STRANGE

INTENT

Nina Bleu

DIVINE WORKS PUBLISHING, LLC.
Royal Palm Beach, Florida

ISBN-13: 978-1-969860-02-7 (paperback)
ISBN-13: 978-1-969860-03-4 (eBook)

First Edition Published: 12/10/2025
Printed: Royal Palm Beach, Florida, United States

Divine Works Publishing books are available at special discounts when purchased in quantity for premiums and promotions and for educational and fundraising use. For details, feel free contact us via email: books@divineworkspublishing.com or call the number listed below.

Published by:
Divine Works Publishing
Royal Palm Beach, Florida USA
www.DivineWorksPublishing.com
561-990-BOOK (2665)

DEDICATION

I dedicate this book to my mother Giovon and my sister Shenora Alicia. I finally completed this after many years of saying I was going to. Rest easy now mommy and Shae.

CONTENTS

The Whisper Between Endings and Beginnings

You ever wonder if the life you have right now could be better? If you were granted a do-over from the beginning, would it make a difference? I once thought I had all the answers figured out but now as I sat here feeling overwhelmed, staring in bewilderment at the final choice awaiting me, laying on the desk in front of me, I questioned everything.

How did it reach this point? How did I allow myself to get so caught up in being right and taking the moral high ground that I couldn't see what was in front of me all along? I am feeling dumbfounded, confused, sad, and mad all at the same time. How was this possible? I broke down, tears rushing as the cruel truth sank in—my best friend had now become my worst enemy.

After taking a moment to gather my composure, it dawned on me that I must now do something that I had promised my mom I would not do—go back to the old me. Cold, heartless, no filter on feelings and not caring about the opinions of others. Yeah, that's right, the old me before I knew love. The old me that would've left years ago and not even invested the time into whatever this was called because it wasn't a marriage, that's for damn sure.

I signed the paperwork after reading over the specifics within the contract. My lawyer advised me to double-check everything to ensure once it is signed, there is no room for going back and forth between both parties. Never was a thought that crossed my mind anyway. I stood up, held my head high, adjusted the red business suit I wore and headed towards the door. One chapter ending and an uncertain new-beginning awaiting me ahead.

Just as I opened the door, one of my oldest best friends, Natalie, had her hand held up to knock on it. "Girl, are you okay?" She looked perplexed as I reassured her, "Yes, I am okay, and it is what it is."

"Uh, oh," she worrily replied "it's starting already, isn't it?" I looked at her in disbelief but deep down I knew what she meant, still I refused to address it. "No, I have no idea what you are talking about lady." I stared at Natalie intently, refusing to acknowledge her remark. Besides, she knows me too well and she was right. I just wasn't ready to admit it, not yet anyway.

Natalie was tall and slender, standing at about 5'8", with a mixture of black and Mexican descent with long, thick hair. She was often the wingman on dates because her beauty intrigued men and sometimes women to come over to our table whenever we would go out. As we walked outside into the cool crisp fall air, I reflected on the past weeks that turned my life upside down. I really need a nice trip to a spa as I tried to wipe the stressful thoughts away in my mind and focus on the meeting with the lawyer.

"Are you going to act like this the whole ride?" A concerned look sweeping over her face. "I am just worried that you are pushing this situation down in the back of your mind and compartmentalizing again. It's not healthy and you know it!" All her words muffled together in my ears like a bad peanuts cartoon segment... whoop whoop Wah Wah Wah.

By the time I could reply we had arrived at the lawyer's office. "Are you ready?" She asked. "I am ready to get this over with." I quickly snapped back, feeling overwhelmed and anxious. The only good thing about this is that his lawyer would be the only one present. He decided it was best not to show up and thought I would be bringing drama to the meeting. So typical of him to dodge the situation and still find a way to blame me.

The lawyer's office indeed showed to be well worth the retainer amount. The walls were off cream paired with wood and silver accents. The building itself was at least ten stories high and was made of all glass. The building was an work of art and as we walked inside the lay out had a serene calmness to it. I am glad that my girl Natalie decided to be with me for support, lord knows I need it.

"Let's get this over with," I said as I sat down in the leather chair. "Agreed, let's get down to business," Naomi, my attorney confirmed as she looked over at me and reached out holding onto my hand. Naomi is, by far, one of the top black divorce attorneys in the Houston area. Her impressive cases were newsworthy, and she was even one of the few consultants that would often be seen on several news panels. I've known

Naomi for more than ten years and we had become close friends so when it was time for someone to represent my interests and assets in this case, it was, as they say, a no-brainer.

As the assets page was being discussed with his lawyer, David, I began to zone out. David was a no-nonsense, cut straight to the point type of person. Tall and athletic looking, he wore the lawyer profession like a glove. The only downside to him was that he was aggressive at almost any cost. This revealed a less than appealing side of his personality and at the same time kept a lot of people on their toes, so to speak. "Are you okay with the assets division part of this?" My mind perked right back up as Naomi reached out to ask me this. "Yes, it's fine," I replied back pretending to care. I really didn't want anything, especially since that meant at some point me and this person would have to cross paths in the future for any changes. Naomi shot back "Are you sure about this?" I looked over at her and just to appease her, I glanced over the summary once again and nothing really stuck out as being not enough. "Yes, I am sure" I shot back looking at her with my tired eyes. "Ok, it sounds like we are good to go here," Naomi confirmed to David. As Naomi handed me the paperwork to sign, she uttered "hey it's over, once you sign this, you don't have to think about him anymore." I met her gaze and thought, I wish it were that easy.

As the meeting concluded, my lawyer took me to the side for a heart-to-heart talk. "How are you really doing?" she asked with concern in her voice. "I am okay, but I have so many thoughts running through my mind, that I haven't had time to process anything. It's like if I stop to think, my thoughts will overrun me." I told her as tears swelled in my eyes. At the same time, Natalie walked over to me and placed her arms around me. "You know you have been trying to outwork your pain" Natalie stated. "That's not healthy, you should take some much-needed time off and process what just happened and heal from it." She was right and I can't keep trying to bury my feelings into work. It never works, and in the end, it just leads to feeling burnt out.

As all three of us walked down the corridor into the elevator, I was thinking of places that I really wanted to go to that would pamper me and give me a much-needed stress relief. "I got it!" I yelled as I stepped off of the elevator. Natalie and Naomi both turned around waiting for what I was going to say. "I am going to Bora Bora!" I knew this would be the perfect place to de-stress and with the all-inclusive packages they have, I would get the most for the money I was about to spend, or rather his money I was about to spend. "Oh yes, that is a good idea," Natalie added, "and you won't have to worry about feeling guilty for leaving your phone on silent." "This is true, Naomi chimed in, and I love Bora Bora islands; it is just something about it that says true paradise."

Walking to the car, I decided to start booking the vacation packages. Since I told my office assistant, Layla, that I would be out of the office for about three months, I could totally do this trip. Usually, he and I would travel together or with a few of my friends. This time though I knew being alone to process and come up with a game plan mentally would be critical to me regaining some of my sanity.

"Natalie, I really appreciate you driving me here, you really don't know how much this means to me." "Girl don't worry about it, I will always be here for you no matter what, just make sure to call me when you get to Bora Bora so that I know you have landed safely."

As she dropped me off at my new place, I waved her goodbye and promised to call her once I set a date to leave for the islands. Once inside, I was reminded that I hadn't unpacked much of anything. Hiring movers was the smart way to go, but who was going to help me unpack? I shook my head as I chuckled to myself.

I did want to keep the house he and I brought together because I was going to rent it out and that would be another income stream for him and I. Obviously, Christian thought selling would be better because as usual he thought his way was the right way. I said his name with a bitter taste in my mouth. In my mind, I refused to address him by his name. The less I thought about him the better. He never thought for the long term, only for the immediate. This always proved to be a difficult issue in our marriage. He didn't believe that I could successfully run a real estate business without throwing money into it constantly. He would ask me consistently how much I was clearing each month and questioned my every decision in the business. I came up with the upfront money to buy the building, to lease the office space to other businesses, and to hire the staff I felt I needed to keep the business running as it should be. He never put any money into it but often would question me as if he had. I often told him I am not one of your clients, you can't interrogate me like I have done something wrong. I will give credit where credit is due, he is a damn good attorney but wound up being a horrible husband. The divorce though came out of nowhere.

I sunk down on the deep red sofa, realizing that our differences had become too great to make the marriage work. We had tried counseling, which he initially refused.

After a few rounds, I thought we were at a good point. He even suggested we get away from both careers for a while and have a nice cruise. That cruise was lovely; he and I talked openly about what was on each other's minds. He didn't like some of the decisions I made but I also pointed out how he often criticized my decisions when I did make them. Our communication styles had always been different, but in the beginning we chose to overlook it, pouring our energy into each other and the goals we believed we shared. I let out a long sigh, realizing that communication styles going forward will matter.

At heart I was a true romantic and I like fairy tale weddings but not fairy tale relationships. No one wants to live forever at Disneyland. Wiping the thoughts of what happened and whose fault it was from my head, I opened my laptop to book the trip. I definitely needed an open bar and food options with this trip. It was not a honeymoon or girls' trip; it was a mental, emotional and much needed unwind time.

As I hit the final button to submit the trip, I instantly felt a rush of excitement I hadn't felt in a long time. The villas on the beach itself were ideal for swimming and for relaxing on a float. I intended to do both.

I glanced at the pile of boxes labeled "kitchen" and "dining room" staring back at me from the corner of the room. I began unpacking and putting away as much as I could. Just in time for more delays, the phone rings and it's Jaden.

Jaden is one of my best friends, we met when I first got into the real estate market. We are both competitive and often did a score card thing with how many houses we closed in a month. I laughed to myself thinking just how much we would compete throughout the years. "Hey lady what's up, "

I chimed into the phone. Jaden stands the same height as me, at 5'5" and curvy with naturally curly hair. My hair naturally curls but not as loose and defined as her curls. Jaden and I went to real estate school together and we have rode together ever since. We were instantly connected as friends and even the friendly competition only cemented our friendship over the years. "Girl, I am going to Bora Bora on his dime." I excitedly told her over the phone. "Oh, that sounds so nice right about now, but I have more than a few clients that are closing at the end of this month". She rolled back of course not meaning to take away from the trip I have but feeling a bit sad because she herself realized she needed a vacation sooner than later. "Lady, please have enough drinks for me; I need to book any vacation at this point". She blasted back into the phone, then stated "Listen, I have a free evening and wondered if you were up to going out to have a few drinks and grab some dinner at our favorite spot". "Yes," I stated almost before she could finish her sentence. "I need to finish unpacking a few more boxes, just text me the time and I will meet you there". I needed this bonding time and needed to go out to get out of being in my head. "Ok" she shot back, and we hung up the phone. Ten minutes later, I received a text from Jaden stating 6: 30pm for meet up.

I think I will drive this time; I mumbled to myself. I then finished unpacking and putting away as many of the items as I could. Lord knows I don't want to unpack for another week. I then grabbed my purse and keys and headed out of the door. I walked to the black Mercedes and opened the door sliding down into the seat. I pumped up the volume on the playlist and proceeded to the restaurant not too far from the condo.

"Ok, I see you, on time for once." I said as I rolled my eyes playfully. I can always joke with her because of our history and ease of friendship. "Girl, you know I don't show up but so late, I can't help it, I have to keep all of this looking soooo good". She hollered back all the while giggling at me. "So did you order our drinks, miss ma'am," she asked. "Yes, I did, I got your usual jack and coke, and I ordered a margarita with light ice."

As if on cue, our waiter came over with the drinks and proceeded to ask if we were ready to order. Yes, we are ready, I chimed in at the waiter. After finalizing our order with the waiter, Jaden hit me on the arm, winking in my direction. I think the waiter was checking you out, she exclaimed in a voice a little above a whisper. I laughed out loud, "girl stop, I am not about to get my get-back with a man young enough to be one of my cousins." I shook my head. Jaden loves younger men and that's good for her, but I am definitely not ready for dating again or even a fling. I am just not at that point in my life, especially after just going through a divorce. What no one talks about is how much you go through, emotionally, mentally and even physically. It makes you exhausted. "Jaden, I appreciate what you are trying to do, but I really need some time to myself, and this vacation is definitely going to help with that." Jaden looked at me agreeing "You are right, I should've considered where you are emotionally and I apologize for that". I shook my head and let her know it was okay and to not worryabout it. "I hope you have the best time in Bora Bora; I truly mean that."

Just in the nick of time, I thought as the waiter came back with our food. "For what you went through in your marriage, I don't blame you for taking a much deserved trip."

Jaden is one of the few friends that really knew what went on in my marriage. Her and Natalie knew when things started to take a left turn and time for me to move on with my life. Those two are what kept me sane throughout this whole ordeal.

"Oh man, this is so good; they better not ever get rid of this dish!" Lobster stuffed ravioli was my favorite dish. I have tried just about everything on the menu, but this was by far what the restaurant was known for. As Jaden and I finished up dinner and discussing the rest of the week, we walked towards each other's cars. "Call me and let me know you got home safe, " Jaden stated as she opened her car door. "I will," I replied back while sliding down into the seat.

On the long drive home, I mentally went through the list of things I needed for the trip before I flew out to the fabulous islands. Then I thought, nothing gives you motivation to lose weight like going through a divorce. I was at a steady size 16 while married but now I have literally lost three sizes and nothing I have really fits anymore. I have a few dresses that are in different sizes, thankfully I didn't donate them all.

Just thinking about that, sends me in a mind-boggling frenzy. I never saw this coming, and people always talk about signs but there were no signs. I will give him that. He was really good at hiding the other side of him. Maybe there were signs there that I didn't want to see. So many unanswered questions.

Walking back into my home, I immediately went straight for my suitcases. Then grabbing the phone, I proceeded to call Jaden. "Hey girl, I am home and getting ready for this feat of packing." I said while sighing because I knew it wouldn't be a lot of clothes but a lot of bathing suits.

"Have enough drinks for me," she fired back excitedly that I was going away and not staying home moping around. "Oh, I definitely will include lots of shots," I said with more excitement as I knew that the trip was just around the corner. "Ok girl, talk to you later and call me once you land, no matter what time it is," Jaden shot back, then she hung up.

Just as I placed the phone down it chimed with a text message from my assistant telling me to have a good time and reassuring me that my backup, Jim, would be showing the two open houses I have coming up and if I needed anything to let her know. Layla, my assistant, has been through the thick and thin of my business and she was an invaluable person of which I always made sure to give her the kudos she deserves. Layla was one of those people like me, always looking at the positive side of any situation. She was my sister from another mother. I mean without having her in my corner, my business would have folded a long time ago. Layla is feisty, standing at just 5 ft tall, blue eyes and dark brown hair. She demanded attention whenever she spoke and was very opinionated. Her being outspoken is why I hired her. She would tell me what I didn't want to hear, and I have nothing but respect for her. As I tucked myself into bed, I thought these nights is when I miss companionship. I missed another person's warmth, their laugh, or even just their breathing—though with my ex, it was usually only the latter. That last thought made me chuckle.

SNAKE BITES

I woke up that morning with purpose, the kind that comes when adventure is waiting. The shower was quick but clarifying, water streaming down as I mentally ticked through my packing list one more time—toiletries, phone charger, my preset playlist. My flight left early enough that the predawn streets would still be empty, so I'd arranged for an Uber to carry me to the airport through the sleeping city. I was more than excited, I was electric with it. It had been far too long since I'd boarded a plane bound for somewhere beyond borders, and even longer since I'd felt that particular thrill of departure. Although I'd tucked my laptop and phone into my carry-on, I'd already made a promise to myself—the moment I arrived at the villa, they'd both go dark. What I needed, what I was craving, was the kind of peace that comes from true disconnection, a chance to unwind without the constant pull of notifications and obligations. My therapist's words, not mine, though I'd come to believe them completely.

The airport wasn't too crowded since it was early in the morning. I made sure to have my passport ready when I approached the international counter. "Next" the TSA agent yelled for the next person to move up. Looking around I never thought about how much it takes to run an airport. The staff, management, security measures; it all seemed to be over-whelming. "Next" yelled the next TSA agent and as I walked up, I noticed a man standing at the counter already. Standing behind him, I heard the TSA agent tell the man in an aggres-sive voice, "Sir, you are not next in line, this lady behind you is." I thought, to myself, I would never want to get on her bad side. As the man apologized to her, she just waved him off. When the man turned around, I looked into strikingly beau-tiful brown eyes. He spoke and I spoke with quick stares of each other. I hurried on and shuffled to the counter.

The TSA agent asked where I was going, why I was going and handed me some paperwork along with a list of items not to bring back from there. She stamped my passport and wished me to a safe flight. This was definitely surprising seeing how she almost cursed out the man that mistakenly walked up. After going through the security checkpoint, I checked in my luggage, hoping and praying it arrived at the same time that I did. I heard horror stories about luggage being lost or worse stolen and then the person would have to scrap together some type of outfits until the luggage was found or delivered. Often when I did travel, I made sure to have outfits that were airport friendly, and this trip was no different. I often dressed in simple jogging pants and a t -shirt and carried a light jacket in case the cabin of the plane was cold. Definitely no sandals, heels, crocs or whatever was the latest fashion these days.

Sitting there waiting for the boarding announcement, I decided to check a few emails and text my friends to let them all know I had arrived at the airport and expected to be leaving within the hour. I then decided to scroll through social media and see what was happening. After about ten minutes, the boarding announcement was called. I looked down at the phone that had my ticket information on it and got into the line. A flash of excitement once again washing over me. Once inside of the plane, I sat down in the comfy chairs and proceeded to put my phone on airplane mode. I noticed myself breathe deeply, finally disconnected and detached.

The flight itself was not as crowded as I thought it would be. An older woman sat down beside me, I noticed her jewelry. It was simple but exotic looking. "Is this your first time going to Bora Bora dear,"she asked with a slightly noticeable French accent. "Yes ma'am, I heard so many wonderful things about the area." I replied to which she said, "it is all true, my dear." Her eyes were a steel gray, and she had blonde hair. Her facial structure was that of a model, but you could tell by her wrinkles that was a lifetime ago. "This is at least my fifth time going to this area"she stated and explained how the first time she went she was blown away by the beauty of the place and had made it her mission at least every five years or so to retu She discussed that her husband and herself would always go but since he has passed away, she tries to continue the tradition of going. "I am sure that he is with you in spirit." I replied back. The conversation then turned to me. "So why are you going here by yourself, my dear?" she inquired because she saw no wedding band on my hand. "Let's just say that this flight isn't long enough to get into that story." I added. "This is the time I need for myself to mentally process and recharge." I seem to do my best thinking around water, but I still have never been able to figure out why. "I understand my dear and unfortunately life is indeed unpredictable." After she said that, she turned around and opened her book. I then decided it was the right time to plug in my ear buds and play my music.

As the flight passed the halfway mark, the gentleman from earlier made his way over and started talking to me. "Hey, I guess we meet again," he said, settling into the seat beside me.

"Yes, it looks that way. Are you going to the island as well?" I asked, finding myself caught in his warm brown eyes.

"As a matter of fact, I am," he replied, then continued, "Is this your first time in this area?"

"Yes, it is. I wish I would've taken this trip sooner." The words came out more nervous than I'd intended, and I realized with a start that it had been far too long since someone of the opposite sex had simply talked to me like this.

"Well, I hope you really enjoy yourself while you're here." He smiled as he stood to return to his seat.

No doubt, sir. No doubt at all, I thought, slipping my earbuds back in.

Music seems to take away a lot of stress for me even better than a therapist could. You can just imagine anywhere within the music your life is and where it is going to. Also listening to older music brings up memories and where you were at in that particular time period. I had fallen asleep and jolted awake hearing the announcement that we were about 40 minutes out from the airport. I sat up and made sure I had everything packed and looked around the plane. Most everyone was asleep and starting waking up. I rented one of the bungalows at this lovely all-inclusive resort. I need everything to be covered, ok. After landing, everyone was standing around and getting their carry-ons and luggage together to walk through the airport. Walking towards the terminal landing, the pilot, co-pilot and stewardess were greeting everyone and wishing them a safe rest of the trip. Walking into the airport felt like walking into another part of the world. The overall atmosphere felt dreamy, no one was rushing, no one was on their cell phones while walking, and just the overall vibe was so positive and welcoming. Feeling the last year of stress lifting off of me as I moved through the airport, I embraced every sight, sounds, and smell. It also felt good to not have to be accountable for another person either.

Once outside a black SUV waited for me with my last name written on the sign.

"Hi, I am here," I waved to the driver, and he proceeded to open the door for me to get into the truck.

"How was your flight ma'am?" He politely inquired after placing my luggage in the trunk and sliding into the driver's seat.

"It was good and long but I got some sleep which was much needed." I replied back.

As the car approached the resort area, I could see the beautiful surroundings of crystal-clear water and white sand everywhere. The trees were a bright green color and luscious with growth. The flowers were an array of vibrant colors, and the place looked like a tropical paradise. The driver pulled into the resort area and the staff were outside waiting to greet me. I felt like a true celebrity. Climbing out of the vehicle, the majestic entrance of the main building was breathtaking. The mansion was a lovely wine color with wooden white shutters and grand entrance doors. The mansion was surrounded by an assortment of flowers. Walking into the grand entrance, I was greeted by one of the attendants of the main house. "Welcome, Ms. Greene, I hope your drive over was a pleasant one." The olive faced woman asked. "Yes, the drive was very nice, thank you for asking." I replied with a smile on my face.

As I continued into the grand foyer, the attention to detail confirmed everything the reviews had promised, This place was extraordinary. White marble floors gleamed beneath my feet, and the brightness pouring through the huge doors and windows made the classic furniture seem to glow, transforming the whole space into something like a wonderland. In the main room just off the hall, I found the front desk alongside an impressive spread of finger foods, drinks, water, and juices. The drinks sat in huge coolers packed with ice, while the food was arranged on white and gold platters atop large wooden tables. The expansive area was framed by arched French doors, and above, the ceilings were lined with slowly turning wooden fans. Through those doors, the view was nothing short of breathtaking. I was still admiring it when one of the attendants who'd greeted me at the entrance gently interrupted my thoughts, gesturing toward the tables. "Ma'am, we have refreshments and food if you'd like to try them," she said warmly. "Also, I'll get you checked in and assign you to your villa."

Following the attendant, I noticed the front desk itself was a work of art—handcrafted wood with intricate carvings running throughout. After checking in and receiving my villa keys, I made my way back to the food table and selected a few items. Everything looked incredible, the presentation alone worth photographing. I settled into one of the chairs and let my eyes wander across the walls. They were covered in wallpaper that echoed the tropical theme woven throughout the resort—a misty rose color embossed with palm trees, all framed by white wood trim accented with gold. The furniture picked up that same darker shade of pink, complemented by dark wood and gold-trimmed tables. Definitely luxurious, and I had to admit it was well worth what I'd paid. I grabbed a bottle of water as I stood, and the same attendant reappeared to walk me through where everything was located. We headed out the back this time and climbed into a golf cart. "If you need anything, just let me know. My name is Sasha," she said as we started moving toward my villa. "Simply contact me through the operator." "Okay, sounds good," I replied.

As we approached my assigned villa, I noticed people walking along the sides of the graveled road. They waved as we passed, and I waved back, pleased to see that the paths weren't crowded. I'd never cared much for packed resorts—there was no true peace in them, no real quiet. You always felt obligated to be present, to engage in conversation and play polite when you'd rather just exist in your own space. When we pulled up directly in front of the villa, I felt a surge of excitement to see inside and finally escape into the water. "Here we are," Sasha announced, waiting as I unloaded my luggage from the cart. I was grateful I'd limited myself to two bags. I couldn't imagine trying to maneuver a cart full of luggage without something toppling off. Sasha helped, of course, but even with just two pieces, anything more would have been a challenge.

As I opened the door, I immediately was greeted by the incredible view of the vast blue sparkling water. The immaculate kitchen had everything I needed without having to travel out to the main house. The stainless-steel appliances included a wine fridge that was fully stocked with all kinds of beer, wine, and liquor. Sasha reminded me before leaving that if I needed anything from the local store, I should just call and she'd bring it by. I thanked her, and she turned to go, closing the door softly behind her. The moment she left, I exhaled. It felt so good to breathe in that saltwater air drifting through the windows. The large living room and kitchen were decorated in light colors with pine wood flooring that ran throughout. When I walked into the bedroom, I found a king-size bed dressed in a blue comforter with matching pillows that complemented the powder blue walls perfectly. A wall-mounted TV faced the bed from across the room, and in the far corner sat a lounge chair beside sliding doors that opened onto an outside shower and patio. I placed my luggage on the bed and began unpacking, tucking things into drawers and the closet. Then I decided it was time to get into the water. I changed out of my airport clothes and into a red bikini. I'd lost so much weight that I had a bit of a stomach now, but I didn't let it bother me. The swim would do me good. I pulled my hair up into a ponytail and walked out onto the patio, climbing down into the water. The coolness against my skin felt incredible in contrast to the heat. The humidity was there but not oppressive. I didn't even bother with sunscreen. I wanted the tan lines, welcomed them, actually. I'd missed being outside without Houston's suffocating heat. Houston had been quite a change from where I grew up in South Carolina, specifically in a small coastal city called Tolly Beach. Living near the water had become part of who I was. The way the sky looked out over the waves, the rhythm of the tides—it was all woven into my childhood. My parents had a mid-size boat, and we used to spend weekends catching fish and crabs.

Those were some of the best times I'd had with my family. We were a big family too—I had two older siblings and one younger than me. Mom always instilled in us that we could do anything no matter what, and Dad gave us our work ethic. Even though we had everything we could ask for, he still taught us to work hard and be proud of what we did. Sitting there, sinking into the calm water, I thought about reaching out to my siblings to let them know I'd arrived safely. I hadn't talked to them much while I was going through the divorce, but I wanted them to know where I was now, how I was doing. Mom and Dad had supported me through everything during that time—I'd even stayed with them when it became unbearable to be around Christian. Dad never did like the man from the first time they met, and that should've been my clue to get out and run like hell. Dad was a good judge of character, but it was too late for me then—I was head over heels in love, and my family knew there was no talking me out of it. One of my older sisters, Deedre, swears to this day she knew something was off about him when I brought him to one of our family reunions. I can still remember that conversation we had, the one that almost turned ugly. "Girl, he acts like he doesn't want to be around us, and we've been nothing but nice to him," she'd said, looking at me with disbelief in her eyes. "Don't pay him any mind. He doesn't like to be around anybody, really," I'd said back. "Toni, no—he keeps excusing himself to take phone calls. What's up with that?" my older sister shot back. "It seems to be a lot of business calls, so to speak," she added, putting her fingers up in air quotes. "Dee, look, I can only go on what he's telling us, but yeah, he should've told his assistant to take his calls while he's with family," I replied, shaking my head because I was just as confused as Dee about why he insisted on answering calls that interrupted our time together. "Girl, you need to talk to him before I do. Something isn't right, and I can tell." Dee said, knowing full well I don't like confrontation but couldn't blame her for how she felt. Come to find out, even then he was entertaining people outside of the marriage. In hindsight, I should've questioned everything he told me. I took it all at face value when I shouldn't have. That's how I ended up in therapy, blaming myself for not seeing the truth staring me in the face. I was the arm candy, nothing more, nothing less. It had taken two years of consistent therapy to reach a place where I didn't blame myself for his shortcomings. Christian, in his mind, thought he was playing a part, but he didn't realize this was real life and there are no parts where what he did was okay. I breathed a deep sigh, letting those memories release into the air as I looked out at the water and watched the sun begin to set. When I finally climbed out, I felt so much better, at least emotionally. It was as if the saltwater had drawn out all the negative doubts and replaced them with peace and positivity. Walking back into the house, I headed to the bathroom to shower and change into something more comfortable. The water had left me feeling energized, and the warm shower washed away the last of the negative thoughts clinging to me. Getting out, I felt more like myself than I had in the past three years. For so long, I'd just been going through the motions, never fully present in the here and now. After I dressed, I walked into the kitchen to see what I wanted to eat. There was seafood, meat, chicken, vegetables—they'd thought of everything when stocking the refrigerator. I grabbed some shrimp from the freezer and placed them in a pan on low heat. While they cooked, I reached into the cabinet for pasta and sauce to pair with them. As the pasta boiled, I heard the vibration of my phone. Funny—I thought I'd turned it off. Picking it up, I saw I'd missed a call from Dee. That girl always knew when I was talking about her, even in spirit. I chuckled to myself and dialed her back. "Dee, I made it here safe. You can tell the rest of the family where I am." "Toni, okay, sounds good. How are you doing, love? You know the family's asking," my sister said. "Oh, it is so beautiful here," I replied. "I don't know if I want to leave." Which really was the truth. I knew it was expensive, but I'd be willing to have my accountant work out the figures and see if I could do business from this end. "I bet it is, girl," Dee said, then continued, "I'm with you in spirit, but I wish I could be there in the physical." "I know, but you know I needed this time to just get away from the hustle and bustle." "I'll keep this short then. I love you, sis, and if you need anything, you know I'm here anytime." Dee hung up, and I stood there missing her more than I'd admit. She was my rock, the one who gave the best advice in any situation. Our parents had taught us self-love at an early age, but me being headstrong had led me into some crazy situations over the years. I could still hear my mom calling me by my full government name when she knew I'd messed up "Antoinette Lisa Greene." I said it to myself now, and a broad smile came over my face. Even through all of that, my mother never gave up on me. When I launched my business, my parents loaned me the startup money, not my former husband. He was too busy trying to make partner at the law firm. Deedre and I were the closest of my siblings, even with three years between us. My oldest sister Patricia—we always called her Trish—was so busy being a surgeon, finishing medical school, that we only saw her around the holidays. She was already in college by the time Dee and I were in high school. Trish was always someone you could talk to, though. She understood the divorce situation better than Dee because she'd been through one herself. Hers was a young and in love marriage. Trish was a sophomore, ready to have a kid and everything from this scumbag she'd met only two months prior. Trish and I still laugh about that mess to this day. She realized that if she didn't get a divorce, he'd still be living off her money like he was entitled to it. Trish told me back then—you'll see the worst side of a person's personality when you go through a divorce. Up until that point, they'll still be putting on a fake personality, acting through the emotions, doing anything to keep you in that bad space. They want you to suffer like they are, but at the expense of your mental sanity. Trish always kept it real with her advice, and that advice helped me see that Christian was such a hypocrite. He did anything and everything to keep me down—emotionally, mentally, physically. Our minds beat us up, replaying the negative on repeat. Therapy wasn't needed for Trish because her situation was slightly different. Her then-husband just wouldn't hold down a decent job, he was who we referred to as Mr. Can't-Get-Right. I think he was only in college to appease his parents. His major was literature with a minor in football, and he wasn't even good at football—definitely not NFL level. Trish met him at the University of South Carolina, but that's where the similarities between them ended. He had a light complexion with striking green eyes. I told Trish not to even look his way when I came to visit her on campus once, and I was still in high school. I knew he spelled trouble. Trish had stars in her eyes, as our parents would say. He just rubbed me the wrong way, and Dee felt the same. We both saw through those pretty eyes to the red flags underneath, and we even threatened him not to play our sister or there would be hell to pay. Our youngest brother, Kevin, even got in his face one day about Trish. Our family didn't play that.

Even with Christian, being in Houston gave him the advantage of not hearing my family in his ear. Trish, in her heart of hearts, knew it too. She got out of the marriage right after she graduated from college—promptly filed for divorce, left him still in school, and went on to medical school in Boston.

As the pasta was boiling, I noticed the shrimp was done. I made the pasta sauce and steamed some broccoli. Dinner was almost ready. I turned on the TV to see what was on and channel surfed until I found a good movie. As I ate dinner, more memories came flooding back. One night, Christian and I were sitting on the sofa when his phone rang. I hadn't heard his phone on an actual ringtone in so long, I didn't know whose phone it was. Christian almost jumped out of his skin as he grabbed the phone and dashed into the other room. Then, peeking back out, he said, "I got to take this." I looked in his direction and turned back around, thinking to myself—surprise, surprise, of course you have to take it as usual. By this point in our marriage, we were just going through the motions, and I started to look for entertainment elsewhere—with friends, acquaintances, male companionship. I never stepped out on the marriage though. It was simple conversations, that's all. I still handled my business, but I wanted to be home less and less, and Christian seemed to be doing the same. I admit, I saw the signs but chose to ignore them. I'd say in our eighth year of marriage, the blatant disrespect I was receiving from Christian was the last straw. I would often pick up the phone and call my mom for advice. My parents had been married for close to forty-five years at that point, and they were still in love with each other as if they'd just gotten married. I never heard my dad raise his voice or talk to Mom in any type of disrespectful way. Never. Mom did admit, though, that when they first got married, she had communication issues due to the way her parents had handled their marriage. Early on, Mom sought help from a marriage counselor and worked on steps to learn to communicate better with Dad, and they've had a strong relationship ever since. Reflecting on the communication issues I had with my former husband, I realized he never mentioned what his relationship with his parents was like. I only met them once or twice the whole time of our marriage. Thinking about that now, it was by design. Who knows what he told his parents about me. Matter of fact, when I first met his parents, I got a very chilly reception from both of them. It felt like I wasn't good enough for him even though I had my own career going on. I attempted several times to contact his parents when it seemed that our arguments were getting out of hand. They never reach out to me or returned any of my calls. If he would call them, they would immediately pick up the phone. I knew then that I was in this marriage on my own. Maybe they knew of his secret and that this marriage was to only appease them and nothing more. So many questions remained unanswered as I snapped out of that memory and began to become sad. Shaking my head, I refused to do so. I am in a tropical paradise now, and I am not trying to go down that road again. I put the food away and cut off the TV. Walking into the bedroom, I shut some of the windows and began to lay down slipping into the comfortable bed. I left one of the windows open to feel the warm air blowing into the villa.

The next morning, as I was getting out of the shower, I heard someone knock on the door. I felt a bit apprehensive because no one knew exactly where I was staying. "Just a minute." I yelled at the door. I hurried up and threw on some clothes and walked towards the door. Opening the door, it was Sasha. "Ma'am I am sorry to disturb you at this hour; we have breakfast at the main house if you would like me to drive you." Sasha said looking very much rested. "Okay, give me a few minutes to gather my purse and make sure I have my key." I replied back but still was feeling somewhat sleepy. I grabbed my purse and made sure to put my key into it. I glanced around the room to make sure I had everything that I needed at that moment. I closed the door and proceeded to join Sasha in the cart.

Once we arrived at the main house, I walked into the area where they had the food prepared and spotted someone that looked familiar. Those familiar brown eyes walked over to me. "Hi, I see we meet again." He uttered and smiled. I bowed my head acknowledging that fact. "Hi, I may as well properly introduce myself, I am Antoinette, but everyone calls me Toni." I said as I shook his hand because who knew when I would see those brown eyes again. "Okay Toni, I am Paul." He replied shaking my hand at the same time.

"Nice to meet you, Toni." He continued. "How are you enjoying your stay so far?" He inquired as we let go shaking hands.

"I love it, the area, the main house, and the weather." I continued "I am wanting to make this place a permanent home; I have to run the numbers though with my accountant." I said jokingly.

"Hey, this place has an effect on people that way." He responded. "Myself, I am here for business, but I love the opportunity to come back just to relax as well." He continued. "I would like to take you to dinner while I am here." He boldly stated.

"Sure, just let me know when and what time. I am here for a week." I shot back making sure to emphasize the week only.

"Sounds good, Toni." He said as he handed me his phone to put my number in. After handing it back, he texted the number, and I grabbed my phone to acknowledge the text. His area code was definitely not from the United States, it was from somewhere overseas.

I moved to grab a sandwich and some pineapple juice for breakfast. In this atmosphere, I didn't feel the need for coffee like I usually did. It was just so bright and sunny, the kind of morning that automatically lifted your spirits. Sitting at the table, I decided to check my text messages. I had a few from my family saying they were glad I'd made it safely to my destination. The usual "I love you" messages from them. I had two from my friends Jaden and Natalie, reassuring me that I hadn't missed anything in the States. I glanced outside and decided to take my food and drink towards the patio. Seems like such a beautiful day not to sit outside. I was kind of excited about the upcoming dinner with Paul. I won't lie—it was refreshing to have someone to get excited about. After swallowing the last bit of juice, I got up and walked back to where I was staying. It was a short walk, so I didn't mind the sun beaming down or the birds chirping overhead.

I decided to get into the water after I got to the villa. I think I wanted to go for a nice swim this time and keep those thoughts away from my mind. I focused on the upcoming dinner date and nothing else. The swim felt so good, the water so warm against my skin. When I swam back to the patio and climbed out, my phone sitting on the table chimed. The text was from Paul—dinner was at 6:30 PM the next day. I replied that it would work for me and giggled to myself. Oh, I had a feeling this would be a good dinner date.

I sat in the chair and thought about what exactly I was going to wear. I decided on one of the sundresses I'd packed. I knew it wouldn't be anything formal or dressy since we were basically surrounded by sand. I'd pair the dress with some nice sandals, I thought. I knew not to get too excited, though. From my past relationships, I tended to be a romantic at heart, giving too many chances to people who didn't deserve them.

My go-to ponytail was out this time. I decided I would braid my hair tonight so I'd have waves for the next day. My hair was currently natural and below shoulder length, which translated to a lot of freaking hair. It was just the right amount of thickness to pull off deep waves, and I was excited, so I started plaiting it into small braids. I was still sitting on the patio, still wet, so I got up and toweled off before going into the house to take a nice shower.

Grabbing a shower cap for the braids I'd just done, I stepped into the steamy shower. It felt so good. I dried off and finished up the remainder of my hair, then made some lunch and sat in front of the TV to check out the local news. Time seemed to fly toward dinner time.

Paul texted me about fifteen minutes before and asked me to meet him at the main house. I was glad we weren't actually going off the resort grounds. I had on a nice yellow, pink, and blue sundress with dark blue sandals that had small jewels on the straps. Walking toward the main house, I turned to the right and entered the dining area. Paul was standing at the table wearing a light-colored polo shirt, a blazer, and some khaki shorts with nice sneakers.

"Hey, I thought it would be best to stay at the resort since there tends to be a lot of traffic outside," he said while motioning for me to sit down.

"I definitely understand since it's a new area for me."

"You look very nice," Paul said while sitting down.

"Thank you." I started looking over the menu to see what I'd like to try. Everything looked so good that I had to narrow it down to at least two choices.

"Do you have an idea of what you'd like?"

"Not really, but I'm narrowing it down and trying to decide. This menu has some of everything on it," I replied to Paul, looking directly at his chiseled face.

"Well, we could always order a sample of everything if you want."

"That sounds good, but would it be too much food between the two of us?"

"Let me ask the waiter if it's possible." Just then, the waiter came back over to the table and clarified that yes, we could have a sample of everything if we wanted, or we could try the best dish the restaurant was famous for.

"Ah, yes, I'd like to try the best dish," I chimed in.

"Okay, ma'am. And for you, sir?" The waiter then turned to Paul.

"Well, since I've been here several times, let me have the best dish for my selection as well." After picking up our menus the waiter proceeded to the back where the kitchen was and put our orders in. The restaurant itself was not crowded but not entirely empty either. It added to the ambience of the restaurant and allowed guests to have somewhat privacy between tables.

We were seated in a booth, and I was deep in thought when Paul started the conversation. "So, I know you haven't been here long, but you must travel throughout the rest of the resort and see the different parts of scenery."

"That does sound like a good idea since I can't exactly spend all day in the water, even though I want to."

"I could show you around after I finish one of my meetings in the morning?"

"Yeah, I would like that."

"Okay I will text you once I finish so you will be ready, what villa number are you staying at."

"Eleven."

"So, are you married, single, or in what the young kids call a situationship?"

I paused slightly before answering, "I am newly divorced. I was married for ten years."

"I was married once myself, but my wife unfortunately passed away about five years ago."

"I am sorry to hear that."

"It's okay, it took me a long time to make peace with not having her by my side."

Out of the corner of my eye, I saw the waiter approaching with the food. The arrangement was artfully done. The waiter set down the platter of dragon-shaped sushi with tuna, salmon, and crab meat selections. "Thank you, it looks very nice," I said to the waiter. Then he placed Paul's food in front of him—a snake-shaped sushi selection with tuna, eel, and lobster. "Thank you, sir," Paul said, and the waiter proceeded to go back to the kitchen. Another waitress came over and asked about our drinks, stating she'd bring them out momentarily.

"In my case, the divorce was a long time in the making," I picked the conversation back up. "We were just on two different plans in life. He made partner at his law firm, but that left little to no time for me. I then started in real estate for the fact that I needed something to do, to not seem like I was ungrateful for being a stay-at-home woman. If I had to speculate, I think he became jealous of my success because he didn't think real estate was worth the risk. Even though he was a partner at a prestigious law firm, he still wanted what I had too."

"Okay, that's a lot, and it seems the better you did, the more jealous he became because it proved to him that you did well without him." Paul had provided the key to what the motivation was with Christian in less than ten minutes of listening than any therapist had done. "Wow, that was pretty insightful," I said.

"Yes, it's very simple. See, he was betting against you instead of with you, like married couples are supposed to do." He paused, then asked, "What have you learned from this lesson?" Paul inquired. "I have learned that if a man has a problem with any recognition that is received to me that is the red flag to RUN."

I laughed out loud as I said it, because it did make so much sense. I had chosen to ignore that simple red flag and ended here on an island with a man that if I had met at the correct time, things would have been different.

After finishing up our food, the drinks arrived and both Paul and I had a merlot wine.

"Will there be dessert?" The waitress asked. Paul took over the ordering of the dessert, which didn't bother me one bit.

"We both would like the chocolate cake to share."

I couldn't have said it better; we had too much sushi to each have dessert.

"Okay I will bring it out once it is ready."

"So, getting back to the conversation, do you have any regrets?" Paul asked.

"I do, but it was more so I stayed in the marriage five years longer than I should have." I answered honestly.

"I figured that the situation of you being here by yourself and not with girlfriends or a significant other was you had just split from someone."

The waitress walked out on cue and sat the cake down in the middle of the table. The cake itself was double chocolate and at least four layers. It, indeed, was big enough to share.

"So, there were signs that the marriage was deteriorating but I suspect you were trying to hang onto it."

"Yes, I was and that was my mistake, and I realized that through therapy."

"Well changing the subject, Paul chuckled lightly, the resort offers scuba diving lessons, and would you be interested in doing that as a follow-up date?"

"Yes, I would, that's an awesome idea." I admitted to him that I love swimming into the water and would like to go deeper to see the corals and sea life.

After finishing up the delicious cake, Paul motioned to the waiter for the bill.

"I really enjoyed this time with you Antionette."

"I enjoyed your company as well."

Standing up, Paul stood right at six feet even. He had a slim build with a bronze tan to his skin. Dark hair made his brown eyes stand out even more. He was truly attractive and definitely had a magnetic personality. He was in his early forties, and he had a few strands of gray hair in his head.

We walked out of the restaurant and walked towards my villa.

"Since it is a bit late, I will walk you to where you are staying. You can never be too careful around here, even with the gated resort."

"Thank you, I appreciate it." As we reached the villa, he reached out and gave me a hug and I felt instant warmth. The hug felt so good, genuinely good and strong.

"Thank you for joining me this evening."

"Okay, have a good night." I turned to open the door.

"I will text you after my meeting tomorrow and also let you know what time the scuba lessons will be."

"Okay that sounds good, goodnight."

As I walked in, Paul started walking back to where he was staying. Shutting the door, I was shaking my head thinking about how good that hug felt. It was the warmth that made me think of him making love to me. He looked like he would be gentle, passionate, and take his time to get to know my body well. That thought made me shiver. I put my purse down and turned off the lights in the living room and kitchen. I then walked into the bedroom and started undressing. My body was on fire from that hug. A feeling that I hadn't felt in a long time. I imagined more than a hug, so I jumped into the hot shower. I then thought of Paul running his hands up and down my body while he was kissing me from behind. As he was kissing my neck, I felt his hardness at the base of my back and into the split of my butt. As I moaned in the shower washing the soap up and down my body, I imagined Paul running his hand over my body softly. It had been years since Christian even bothered touching me. I imagined him thrust himself into me. It was gentle but forceful at the same time. The pleasure and slight pain was too much to stand. This intense pleasure was just right, and I wanted this all of the time. As I was climaxing, he forcefully clinched himself as I felt his pleasure rise as well. Oh, you are so good, I whispered to myself. Oh, oh, aw, oh, I was whispering to myself as my orgasm ripped throughout my body. Whew, I turned off the shower and started wiping down my wet body and wetness. That was better than any sex toy I used. I laughed to myself. That felt so good, and I knew I wasn't even ready for that level of intimacy from Paul yet. I barely knew him for two days. The imagination and thoughts, however, had other plans.

I fell into the bed and ended up in a deep sleep still dreaming of that love making session that I was desperately curious about. The next morning, I awoke to a good morning love text and the details of the scuba diving lessons. I thought to myself well, I'm glad I made a good impression on somebody. I replied back and proceeded to get up and get dressed. His text stated the meeting would be over by eleven o' clock and that would be perfect for meeting up for breakfast. I decided to dress in blue shorts and a light green tank top. The sandals I had on this time were buckled at the ankle and were more comfortable for walking around than the ones I had on the previous evening.

I lounged around on the sofa for a bit since I had some time to waste until Paul's meeting was over. I really didn't want this trip to end. It was truly paradise and none of the busyness of following up on clients, checking on open houses, or constant listing updates that were snatched up just as fast as they were added. I mean it literally was another world on this side of the water. I didn't want to start reaching out to my assistant just yet. I didn't get any text from her which meant good news and things were being handled while I was away. I watched a bit of TV but then decided to sit outside on the patio reading a book I meant to have finished a long time ago. I also made some coffee so I could enjoy that along with the book. The hour was approaching towards eleven, so I finished up the coffee and walked back into the living room putting away the book. I glanced down at the chime on my phone from Paul's text. It stated he was heading towards my villa to pick me up. Making sure I had everything; I glanced around the inside. I heard a knock at the door, and I walked towards it and opened the door.

"Hi, are you ready?" Paul asked, this time looking better than he had last night. He had on a fedora and some linen shorts and a nice pale colored shirt.

"Yes I am." I walked out of the door, turning around and locking it. He had one of the carts that the employees had. "Oh, I didn't know these could be rented?"

"Yes, for the right price of course." Getting into the cart, I put my purse in my lap and held on as he proceeded to drive towards the main house. "I have to stop by the main house to get something. Then we will go a little further to a nice café located adjacent to the main house."

Riding to the main house, Paul parked the cart and went inside. A moment later, he returned and proceeded to drive to the café that he was talking about. The sun was beaming down and not a cloud was in the sky as I looked up and all around taking in the scenery.

"Here we are." I looked to the right and there was a small brown building towards the beginning of the resort area. It had dark brown wooden shutters and was trimmed in a stucco light brown color. Getting out of the cart, we walked into the building together. The place inside was a little busy but not crowded as it only had a small selection of tables and chairs. Walking up to the counter, Paul stated he knew what he wanted, while I glanced at the menu board above the area. I decided to get a selection of local fruit and a bagel with cream cheese. Paul had gotten eggs and bacon with toast on the side. As we sat down at the table, we engaged in small talk.

"So, are you mentally relaxed and stress free?" Paul started off the small talk.

"Yes, I feel like I am more focused on what is to begin the next chapter of my life."

"That's good and that is what you needed to get from this vacation."

"Yes, I needed this time away more than I liked to admit. I know sometimes we as a people can be stubborn to changing our surroundings, our view, and it can lead to some health issues if we continue to not do anything about it."

Finishing up our food, we walk outside and decide to walk to the beach since it was such a beautiful day.

"I am going to be honest; I meant to cut the line when I spotted you at the airport. I was attracted to you from that point on and when you were open to conversation; I figured this is what was meant to occur."

I was slightly taken aback, but in a good way. I was flattered because I never met anyone who intentionally tried to get my attention. He continued. "I knew it was a risk, but I figured the worse you could do was tell me you weren't interested." It has been a long time since I felt feelings of attraction so soon. I had to question myself if this is right or am I just forcing myself onto her. Deep down, I knew it was time for me to move on from my wife. I just had so many conflicting emotions about it.

"Well, I am glad you were honest with me. I am flattered that you initiated the conversation, because to tell you the truth, my mind was a million miles away on the airplane. I am recently divorced though and at this point in time, I am not looking for a relationship or anything ending with the word ship."

"Okay, I understand that, and I can do nothing but respect that choice. I am going with the flow for you, but I just wanted you to know how I felt about you. I would love to become intimate with you, but that is only if you are comfortable with that idea. It doesn't have to lead to anything or if you want it to be more, just let me know.

We were both standing in the sand at this moment, having reached the beach sooner than I thought we would. I noted to myself that time seemed to fly whenever I was with him. I ran the scenarios in my head of what sleeping with him would mean for me. It had been more than five years since my former husband and I had any type of sexual involvement. We only recently officially divorced but the marriage was physically and emotionally over five years ago.

"Let me think it over." I wanted Paul to know that if we did sleep together, it wasn't going to be on this trip. Maybe I will see him again or maybe I won't. At this point, I had my mind made up that it would happen when I see him again. If it was meant for us to see each other again.

"Okay. Like I said, I can only respect your decision."

"We approached the shoreline of the beach and just stood there with the water going between our toes. I wanted to lean into him for comfort of just being there, but I thought better of it. I didn't want to send the wrong signals that this could be more than it was when I knew I was ready for that. So, you have one more day, correct? Yeah, this time has gone by so fast, it is unreal. We stayed out on that beach standing there with the water on our toes for at least two hours. It just felt so right being around him. Call it divine intervention. Maybe he is what I need to get myself back into where I am dating but just not serious yet. I continued to mull over the negative and positive thoughts in my head, knowing deep down I really wanted to feel his kiss, touch, and closeness. In my mind, what could it hurt to just have a fling with him, no harm no foul.

Interrupting my thoughts. We should head back to the villas. Paul started and put his hand gently in the small of my back and we walked back to where we were staying. Once we reached my villa, I turned around to unlock the door. As I turned back around, he suddenly leaned in and kissed me. It was a light kiss, gently on the lips. The electricity sent shockwaves through my body. Then he gently backed up and let go.

"I had a good time today with you. Thank you for your company. Here I was thinking this was going to be a typical work vacation with boring meetings. Hopefully I can see you tomorrow before you board your flight."

"Uh, yeah I think I will have time to see you before I have to be at the airport," was all I could get out after the shock from that kiss to my system.

"Great, I will see you then, have a good rest of the evening." I then turned back around going through the door. I kept shaking my head as I walked into the living room and the sun was just beginning to set in the background. I proceeded to start packing the clothes I knew I wasn't going to wear on the flight back. I left out one swimsuit, thinking I might get in an early swim before showering. As I looked around the villa, making sure I had most of everything packed, I received an incoming text with the flight information and gate. Then I saw another text from my oldest sister, Trish. She wanted to know if I needed a ride from the airport to my home. I replied yes, that hopefully I'd arrive back to the States on time, pending any flight delays.

Trish and Leon had decided to come see me for the holidays. She wanted to help me finish unpacking from the move, and Leon, I'm sure, just wanted to see the new eighty-inch TV I'd mounted in the living room. They were helping me host the upcoming Thanksgiving and Christmas holiday with the rest of the family. They'd flown into Houston yesterday to be there in time to pick me up from the airport the day after tomorrow. Of course, I had a slight adjustment to go through with the time zone being ahead almost a day over here in Bora Bora.

I was so glad that Christmas was still at least three weeks away because I was already dreading being the hosting house for this year. It could get overwhelming, especially now that Christian was no longer in the picture. However, now that I thought about it, he'd never been into holiday celebrations anyway. He tried to duck out of them by being at work or at the local bar. Even when he was around, he wasn't really around. Pushing that thought out of my mind, I decided to channel surf and make something to eat.

I'd timed this vacation just right. It was literally summer on this side of the world, while it was winter in Houston— well, as best as winter could be in Houston. We didn't really get a lot of cold weather like that. At best it was a balmy forty-five degrees, and that was chilly compared to home. We didn't get any snow, but we definitely had winter-like temperatures, especially in January and February. I surfed the channels for a bit while eating my food, still thinking about how that kiss felt between Paul and me. I knew he'd felt that electricity between us, it was hard to miss. I put the food in the trash and made sure no leftovers were left in the fridge or the freezer. Since this was officially the last night, I decided to open the liquor and pour a drink. I really hadn't drunk as much as I'd thought I would on this trip. The surroundings were just so stress-free that I hadn't had the desire to drink until tonight. The anxiety tried to creep up, but I brushed it to the side. I didn't need that trying to mess up what little time I had left.

I grabbed my phone and sent Trish my flight information so that in case it got delayed, she could call the airport for updates. She texted me back that she loved me and to have a safe flight. I decided to call it a night earlier than usual since being here. I knew I wanted to get up early so I could get a last swim in and then meet Paul for breakfast at the main house. I settled into bed, and not long after, I was in a deep sleep.

Waking up the next morning, I couldn't believe how fast time had passed. I changed into my swimsuit and dove into the water. It felt so cold and refreshing, I didn't even want to think about leaving today. Everyone here was so friendly and polite. It was really hard to think about going back to the States. I swam around for another thirty minutes, then got out and headed toward the shower. After taking a nice long shower, I put the swimsuit away in an airtight plastic bag made for wet items; the best investment I'd spent money on. I put on some clothes that were comfortable for the flight home.

Paul texted me a good morning message and said he'd be at the main house in another twenty minutes. I replied that I'd meet him there. Since it was my last day, I'd contacted Sasha to come so I could take my luggage with me. About ten minutes later, Sasha arrived and pleasant as usual she assisted in placing the luggage on the cart.

"How was your stay?" she asked.

"It was everything I dreamed of for a vacation. I will truly miss this place."

"Well, you have to come back and see us sooner rather than later."

"You're right. When I get back to the States, I'll start planning when I can come back—maybe stay longer than I did this time." Since this trip was funded by my ex-husband's alimony, I knew I'd be able to splurge more on my dime than his.

"Ahh, here we are, ma'am, at the main house."

"Thank you, and I really appreciate all that you did to provide me with the best experience on this vacation." I waved bye to Sasha and walked into the main house. Another gentleman took my luggage and informed me they were going to take it directly to the airport, so all I had to do was scan my ticket once I got there. That was great to hear—it could be a bit much toting luggage around.

I chose a few items from the breakfast spread and picked a seat to sit down in. I was tempted again to sit outside, but that only made the agony of leaving worse. I picked up a plate of eggs, steak, and a fruit plate on the side. Looking toward the open hallway, I saw Paul wave, and after picking up his food, he walked toward the table.

"Good morning. Last day of vacation." I immediately chuckled, thinking about the long flight ahead. He laughed back.

"I'm here about three days longer than you, so I know how you're feeling. I was trying to get the company I work for to extend my vacation, but they declined instantly."

"Well, I mean, you really can't blame them. It is on the expensive side for any company's bottom line."

"Yeah, I know." He paused, then said, "You have my contact number. Please don't be a stranger once you get back to the States."

"I won't." I then looked into his eyes as I said, "I am not quite ready for a relationship or situation but I want to take you up on the sleep offer."

He nodded, understanding what I was referring to. "Okay I will check my calendar and give you a few dates that will work for me."

"Okay that sounds like a plan." As we continued eating and talking, I kept checking the time for me to arrive at the airport. We talked for what seemed like hours but only twenty minutes had gone by.

Standing up, he walked over to me and gave me a long hug. It felt so good in his arms and made me feel better on my decision knowing what was to come up. He then walked with me to the main door and we exchanged goodbyes. Another attendant drove up in a SUV that was to take me and a few others to the airport. I climbed into one of the back seats of the truck and after the others were loaded into the vehicle, I waved again to Paul and a sadness came over me that I hadn't felt in a while. I really was going to miss him. His friendship and knowing the island and everything it had to offer was helpful in me being there by myself.

3

STIRRED UP SECRETS

Once I arrived at the airport, I climbed out of the SUV and made my way to the check-in station. I scanned the ticket, and the worker behind the counter stamped my passport.

"Enjoy your flight," she said. I nodded and walked down to the area where passengers were waiting to board.

"Now boarding international flight E24 from Bora Bora to Houston, Texas, United States." I heard the boarding call and got in line with the rest of the passengers. I looked around and noticed the flight was definitely lighter than it had been flying here. I had my phone in hand so the attendant could rescan my flight information.

Walking onto the plane, I found my assigned seat and put my earbuds in to listen to some good music. This flight was going to be a while. I got as comfortable as I could and fastened my seatbelt. I fell asleep, and it must've been for quite a while because I woke up and realized we were already entering United States territory. The pilot announced there was slight turbulence due to several storms sitting over the eastern part of the country.

"Ladies and gentlemen, I don't want to alarm you, but we are experiencing some bumpy weather in the area. Please fasten your seat-belts," the captain continued. "I'll keep you posted when we've moved through these wind pockets." I hadn't realized I'd taken my seatbelt off, but I must have to lie down more comfortably. We'd gone through most of the flight, so I wasn't tired anymore and was ready to get home safe and sound. I was definitely glad this time I hadn't chosen a window seat.

"Ladies and gentlemen, we have resumed calmer weather, so you can unfasten your seat-belts." I was okay at the moment and left mine on. I turned on my internet since we were still at a safe altitude. I'd had my cell on airplane mode most of the flight because I knew I'd be asleep while most of my family was back in the States. Now, looking at social media, I didn't miss that week-long break from it. It really was a time sucker. So I decided to just find a movie on one of the sites and watch that for the rest of the flight.

Waking up again, I realized we'd arrived in the United States. We were almost to the Houston area as the pilot's voice boomed over the PA system.

"Ladies and gentlemen, we are about forty-five minutes away from the airport. We are right now in a holding pattern on standby due to several takeoff flights being behind sched-ule." Well, that was all I needed to hear. I took my movie off pause and kept watching. It felt like an eternity had passed, and my movie was almost at the end when I noticed we were starting to land. Whew, finally, I thought to myself. I knew my family was waiting for me at the airport, and I couldn't wait to see them. It had been several years since I'd seen Trish and her husband. We often talked when we could over the phone, but it definitely wasn't the same.

I hung up my phone and gathered my personal belongings. Still feeling high off my vacation, I spotted Trish and Leon. After picking up the luggage, I walked toward them and gave them both a big hug.

"Aw, it is so good to see you."

"Yes, it has been way too long, Trish.

"Hi, Leon."

"Hey there, Toni. How are you holding up? How was your vacation? I hope you took some pictures." All three of us hugged each other because they knew what that hellion of a man had put me through.

"I'm glad to be back, but it was really hard to leave at the same time." Leon gathered my luggage, and all three of us walked outside to where the vehicle was parked.

"We wanted to respectfully not bug you while you were out there and at the same time give you the time needed to process what you just went through."

Trish understood me so well, we really should've been twins, but Mom had other plans. Leon loaded the luggage into the silver SUV they'd rented while out here visiting me.

"I appreciate it, Trish, and I know you wanted to call before then. I understand, trust me." As we drove up in front of the condo, I noticed I had holiday decorations on the outside of the house.

"Oh, wow, this looks nice, but did you guys do this?"

"Yeah, I hired someone to put up the outside decorations, and me and Leon took care of the inside." Trish knew my taste, so I was overwhelmed to say the least. It looked so good that tears almost came to my eyes.

"Ah, thank you, big sis. I hadn't even thought that far ahead to put up decorations yet."

The condo was located in a gated community and had tan brick with tan siding. It was, as they say, cookie-cutter, but the decorations really took it up a level. Trish would never know how much I appreciated her and Leon doing this. Pulling into the garage, we got out and walked into the house. Once inside, all three of their kids came up and hugged me. Tara and Tasha both said they missed their aunt, and one wanted to know if she could stay through Thanksgiving and Christmas and go back to her parents for New Year's. I nodded. I'd love for her to stay and asked her to check with her parents to make sure it was okay. I knew my work schedule would be lighter than usual due to the holidays, and I knew Tim wouldn't mind showing houses if there were any last-minute changes in the schedule.

"Aunt Toni, I want you to know that Tara and I decorated the tree. Timeka didn't help us at all."

"She didn't? Are you sure about that?" Trish chimed in, knowing what Tasha was up to. She knew that Auntie Toni would give out money for them helping out with the decorations. At that moment, Timeka was upstairs playing on the laptop and didn't hear them plotting behind her back.

"Yes, Mom, she didn't help us at all, and you know she didn't." Looking at Tasha and back at Trish, I knew that child of hers was lying or attempting to lie. I saw right through it and yelled for Timeka to come downstairs.

Just then, Timeka walked downstairs wearing long skinny jeans and an orange long-sleeve top. The kids had all gotten so tall since I'd last seen them. I almost didn't recognize her. Her hair was brushed up into a bun with short curls at the end. Her slender face had some extended eyelashes on, and pink lip gloss. She stood at least five-eight and was the youngest of the siblings. The other two were shorter than her and clearly jealous that she'd ended up with her dad's height. Leon stood easily at six-three and towered over Trish. She was the oldest but the shortest of us at just barely five-one. She always used to tell us growing up that good things come in small packages. We'd often laugh at that saying.

My family was all over the place when it came to height. Mom and Dad were both tall, and how some of us ended up on the lower end of the height spectrum was a mystery only genetics could solve. For instance, Dee was taller than me by two inches, and I was taller than Trish. Kevin, the youngest of us, was the tallest in the family at six-five. His only child, Donte, took his height, and Kevin would brag about this, making sure Donte was in all of the sports. Donte was eight years old and already playing football and baseball. I'd told Kevin it was good for his son to have an outlet but not to look at his son as a future professional player or a check.

Glancing at Timeka, I asked her about what her sister had mentioned earlier while she was upstairs.

"Uhh, no, she's lying. I did participate, and Tasha knows it. She's just being greedy because she wants to buy the new PlayStation." That's what I thought. I gave her a hug and told her I loved her. I gave each of them one hundred dollars for helping their mom and dad.

"Now you know they don't need all of that money," Trish said.

"It's okay. I know how hard they worked to get this house together and even put away a few of the boxes I didn't get a chance to unpack. You've got to reward these kids today for at least making the effort," I chuckled.

Trish and I walked into where the television was in the living room and sat down. Leon was upstairs in the hall area looking at the football game. I usually partook in the football season, but this time I needed to watch some feel-good Christmas movies. The kids were trying to bake some cookies and were glued to their phones.

"Trish, I can never thank you enough for doing all of this and having it so organized by the time I got here."

"That's what big sisters are for. Now what's on your mind, and did you meet anybody while you were over there?" As usual, she was ready for the gossip in my life.

"I did meet someone, but I'm not looking for anything, and you know this. I told him that as well, but he still gave me his phone number."

"The place itself, Trish, was so amazing. From the décor at the main house to the beautiful surroundings. I mean, you literally didn't want for anything."

"Well, that's good to hear, and I need to know more about this man you met."

"He was a total gentleman, and when we kissed, it seemed like time stood still."

"Ewww, I heard that. That's those sparks flying," Trish said dramatically. Both of us burst out laughing. "

"His name is Paul. He stands a little over six feet, and he has such a warm personality."

"Alright now," Trish chimed in. "Sounds like he could have potential. Look, I know you don't want anything right now, and I'm in no way trying to rush you. I just want you to be happy, and whatever you decide this is between him and you, I'll support you."

Trish really was happy for me and had always been the rock of the family. I had to decide, though, if I was able to be happy for myself. Deep down inside, I knew this could be the start of something good. Tasha just then walked into the room and told us the cookies they'd baked were ready. This was what I'd mostly missed—the family—talking, laughing, and just enjoying each other's company. We all got busy with our lives and careers and fell into this rut of focusing on that instead of being around family to keep us strong.

My cell started ringing, and it sounded foreign for a minute. It was my other sister, Dee. Picking up the phone, I said hello.

"Hey, you're home finally," Dee laughed into the phone.

"Yes, I am. When are you guys coming in to see everyone?"

"I know Trish is there already, but I'm waiting on Tim to confirm his days off so we can fly out soon."

"Okay, so basically on Thanksgiving."

"Yeah, it's looking that way. I already have someone covering my work during this time, so I'll be all in once we get there. I can't wait to see you, Toni."

"I feel the same way, Dee."

Hanging up the phone, Trish asked when they were coming in. I turned around and told her they couldn't get in any sooner than the day of Thanksgiving thanks to Tim's schedule. She nodded and said, "Well, I'm just glad we're all going to be here together." I nodded back but wasn't sure how I felt about having to send a driver the day of the holiday to pick up the rest of the family from the airport. Our parents took a direct flight from South Carolina and should be in sometime tomorrow. Thankfully, they'd call us when they got in so Trish and I could pick them up. Dee and Tim were definitely cutting it close, and it almost seemed as if Tim had purposefully planned his schedule to be full, I thought to myself. I mean, come on, who has a full schedule of clients around the holiday time? Personally, I knew Tim wasn't that good of a lawyer, as I'd found out from my own lawyer. People in that industry talked, and there were some not-so-nice things said about Tim.

As Trish and I sat to enjoy the rest of the movie, we started some small talk about what changes had occurred within the family.

"So, with the divorce out of the way, how are you mentally feeling?"

"Honestly, I'm the happiest I've been in a long time, especially around this time of year. Christian, in his mind, thought he was breaking me down by not letting me see you guys as much. His family wasn't close at all, and they never celebrated holidays—you could tell."

"Yeah, I never liked him. Leon and I just wanted you to be happy, which is why I accepted the way he acted around us." "Oh, I thought you really got along with him."

"No, I faked it. I thought he was a scumbag, and I saw right through his perfect façade. He talked a good game, but I've had acquaintances and friends who let me know he wasn't good enough for you."

My mouth dropped upon hearing this news because, as far as I knew, Trish and he seemed to have the most things in common and often joked together. This was a genuine shock. "I never told you this, and you cannot repeat what I'm about to say, not even to Dee. He tried to fake that he'd injured his knee one time and requested his doctor refer him to Leon." Trish's husband was a physical therapist and had worked with all sorts of celebrities and upscale clients. "Leon told me Christian walked into the office, hoping he would spring his knee. Leon and he began to talk about how the injury occurred, and Leon told him to show him where it was giving him problems. So as he points to the area, Leon begins to request an X-ray of the joint to determine if it's indeed a fracture or a muscle tear. Leon walks out of the room to talk with his assistant, and then when he returns, he notices that Christian is lying on the exam table with nothing but the cloth cover-up on." "WHAT? Wait, WHAT?" I could've sworn I didn't hear her clearly when she said what she said. "Yes, I was just as shocked when he told me the story as you are right at this moment. Leon immediately asked him what he was doing and that this was very unprofessional. Leon came home that night furious that Christian would even consider him in that way and who knows who else would've come in with Leon to see this. He said all Christian did was apologize and leave the room. Since then, Leon refused to be in the same presence as Christian, and that's why we never asked to come over to see you during the holidays. Toni, that man was evil, and I'm glad you got to see that yourself before it was too late. Not only did Christian disrespect my marriage by doing that stunt, but he disrespected Leon as a man."

I just sat back farther into the sofa, looking shocked at all of this. I'd had no idea.

"I had to force Leon to tell me what happened because

he was so angry and also ashamed. He always talks to me about anything, Toni, and I knew something was up when he came home that day."

"I have no words. I'm sorry for what happened. I had no idea, and please apologize to Leon for me." Thinking to myself, I knew they hadn't just chosen to stay away from seeing me. I knew something wasn't right, but I couldn't figure out what. "That reminds me of the time he tried to insert himself as cosigner on my business accounts without my knowledge. The bank promptly called me while he was there to let me know that he was trying to request some funds, but in order to do that, he had to be an authorized user on the account." "Girl, I immediately told the bank no, and I would not allow him as an authorized user. He was mad at me for a long time, almost like a kid that throws a tantrum when they don't get their way. Then there was the time that he claimed he forgot to pay the mortgage, and they contacted me directly requesting the funds since we were two months behind."

"Wow, for real?" Trish asked, now with a shocked look on her face. "Yes, I had to take some money out of our emergency fund to pay them. I confronted Christian because, as a woman, if you as a man state you'll handle all the bills, that's what I expect you to do."

"Right. I'm sorry you had to go through that and so much more. The lying, the manipulation, and the emotional toll it took on you. I think he secretly hated you."

"He probably did, but because he's so manipulative, he thought he was playing with my mind. It took a while for me to look at myself in the mirror. My sales began to suffer and almost destroyed my career. If I didn't have friends who kept telling me to leave, I don't think I would have until I was down to almost nothing emotionally and mentally."

"Toni, I knew you were in trouble, and in the back of my mind I wanted to come here and force you to leave him, but Leon was like, 'No, she has to see it for herself and want to make that change.'"

"I totally understand, Trish. Leon was right. I had to get to a point where I knew I'd done all I could and was still made out to be the villain."

We just looked at each other and hugged for a long time. Tears streamed down my face because all this time I thought I'd done something to keep the family away, when it was Christian the whole time. It was ironic now because he would tell me that my family didn't really love me and that's why they didn't want to see me anymore. By the time he kept saying that, I was too low to even fight about it. I'd basically given up, and deep within, I'd wanted to end this pain I was going through. Just then, Timeka came into the living room and brought in some cookies for Trish and me to share.

"Oh, it's nice to finally be waited on for once," Trish teased her.

"The cookies turned out really well. Not bad for first-time bakers," I added.

"Yeah, Tasha read the instructions while me and Tara mixed it up and put them in the oven. We had to wait a long time for them to cool so we could put the icing on." Heading upstairs, Timeka and Tasha screamed at their dad and started bugging him. I laughed to myself as I heard their dad fussing at them for interrupting his football game.

"Those two are forever their dad's babies. They always find some way of bothering him. It doesn't matter what he's doing," Trish said.

Tara came into the living area and started watching the movie we were looking at. "Trish, you did a wonderful job with these girls. I know you guys are worried because I can tell now they're heartbreakers at their schools."

"Right, and you know Leon and I don't play about that. We're not ready to be grandparents, and Mom and Dad may be ready for great-grands, but we aren't." She stared intently at Tara. "What? I know, Mom." Tara went back to watching the movie while texting someone on her phone. "Girl, I can only imagine," I laughed out loud. "Leon is going to give anyone trying to date his daughters hell." "

"Oh, trust me, he has with Tasha's so-called friend now. He came to the house at least like a gentleman and asked her dad for permission to take Tasha out on a date. We've met with his parents and everything. So he knew from the jump to come correct, or there would be no date."

"I know that's right," I agreed.

I'd wanted kids for a while now but was sure glad I didn't have any with Christian. The thought of how ugly that custody battle would be made me shudder with anxiety. All of the things I'd gone through with him—kids would've just made it even harder to leave, that's for sure. I knew at the right time and with the right person, kids would come into the picture. Brushing that thought from my mind quickly, I looked down at my phone. It was Mom and Dad calling.

"Hey, Mom, it's finally good to hear your voice. How's Dad doing?"

"We're fine, and I called you to let you know that we'll be there around one o'clock tomorrow afternoon at the airport."

"Oh, okay. Trish and I will be there ready to give hugs and kisses."

"We love you guys," Mom whispered into the phone.

"We love you too," I chimed back and then hung up. "Mom says she loves us, and we're picking them up at one o'clock tomorrow from the airport."

"Okay, I'm glad we'll be seeing them tomorrow. I'm ready for some of Mom's cornbread and soup," Trish said and smiled from ear to ear at the thought.

"You always loved that combination. I just like the cornbread itself—or more like cake bread." We both laughed. "With that being said, I'm going into the kitchen to fry fish and fries."

Walking into the kitchen, I proceeded to make dinner and was glad I'd taken out some extra food before I went on the trip. I had at least six people here this time, not just me. The cookies, though, were a nice touch from my nieces, and I'd forever love them for that. I looked at my phone and realized I'd received a text from Paul. It said he missed me and wanted to know when I'd like to see him again. Also, he said since he was in the U.K., he would fly me over to see him. I replied back that it would be nice and that I missed him too. I knew I wanted to see him after the holidays were done. I replied back that March would be a good time, usually that was when the business either slowed down or started to ramp up with potential buyers. He texted back, "It's a date." I didn't even think to tell the family much about him. I wanted to see where this could go first.

Turning back to the food, I started on the fries and was almost finished with the fish. Running into the kitchen, Tasha sat at one of the chairs, waiting for the fish.

"I see this is what got you from upstairs bugging your dad to death," I turned to her.

"Yes, you know I love some fish. I could smell it upstairs, and it smelled so good," she said, shifting in the chair.

"It's almost ready." I yelled into the living room that the food was ready and loud enough so Leon and Timeka could hear me upstairs. Everyone started gathering in the kitchen, and Trish grabbed some paper plates from the pantry. As we were sitting around eating, I noticed it felt good to have some voices in this house. I felt the love and warmth from my sister and her family as if eight years hadn't passed since I'd seen them. It warmed my heart that they didn't hold any grudge against me for what Christian had done.

Leon got up to grab another piece, almost beating Tasha to the counter.

"Thank you, Aunt Toni, for cooking this food," Trish said, and everyone nodded while still eating.

"Well, I know once Mom and Dad come in tomorrow, we won't need to make anything else." Mom, bless her heart, would literally take over the kitchen, and Dad would try to assist. My assistant had made sure to pick up everything for Thanksgiving food-wise while I was out of the country and pack it in the freezer. I went into the washroom and began to move the food from the freezer to the refrigerator. I knew it would be a lot of food to defrost from the deep freeze. I'd told Mom and Dad several weeks ago to make a list, and I'd have everything they needed here for their arrival. Trish had brought in her famous lemon pound cake, and I was tasked with making sweet potato pies. Dee would be cooking her potato salad and the honey-baked ham. She liked to have pineapple and cherries on top. I just hoped Dee and Tim got here early enough for the ham to cook and cool in time to be served.

Just then, my phone vibrated, and I received a text from Paul. He was just checking in on me to make sure my family had made it safe into town and that I had everything I needed for the upcoming holiday. I texted him back, and I was beginning to think this guy was growing on me. However, since I'd just gotten out of a marriage, I didn't want to put all my options in this one person. I wanted to keep my options open. As a smile spread on my face, Trish picked up on it and asked who that text was from.

"No one but Paul," I smirked.

"Uh-huh, I see. I'm glad you're at least smiling. I haven't seen that on your face in forever."

"Yeah, I know. It's strange because I've only known him for a short time, and he's growing on me."

"I understand, I do. I want you to keep your options open to other people."

"Yeah, we definitely agree on that. I want to give myself some more time to heal before I get back into the dating pool."

"I'm glad you're on the right path there. That way you won't bring the issues and baggage from the marriage into any potential relationships."

"Right. I figured the more time I have before deciding to date someone, the better."

Changing the subject, Trish talked about how each of her kids was doing in school. Both Tasha and Tara were straight-A students, and Timeka was on her way to having the same GPA. All of them were on the honor roll, and at least the youngest wasn't even thinking about boys yet.

"Aw, Trish, I know you're so proud of them."

"Yes, Leon and I definitely are proud of how much they excel in everything they do. We guide them a lot, especially with social media and how there are people who get pleasure from bullying online. We also tell them not to tolerate that in school because there can be some mean people out there."

"Girl, we're just starting to get through the teenage years. Thank you, God." Both of us burst out laughing. I could only feel what both of them had to go through. I really wanted children, but timing was everything.

Timeka and Tara said goodnight and went upstairs. Leon then got up and started doing the dishes.

"Leon, you don't have to do that. I can get them."

"No, Toni, you cooked, and besides, Trish wouldn't stop fussing at me the whole night if I didn't do the dishes." Trish and I both laughed again because that was true. In their household, if Trish cooked, then Leon would wash the dishes, and vice versa. I liked that myself. Thinking back, Christian wouldn't cook, but at least he did the dishes. I didn't even think he knew how to cook anything. I never questioned it because I liked to cook. Leon finished washing the dishes and said he was going back upstairs to see what other sports games he could watch.

I had three extra bedrooms, so there was more than enough room for everyone who wanted to come over and stay. Once Mom and Dad arrived, they'd take up one of the bedrooms, and then Dee and Tim would take the other bedroom if they didn't decide to stay in a hotel this time. I knew Dee usually wanted to stay in the house, but Tim often didn't like to. Since they hadn't visited since my divorce, I was in a much smaller house, and Tim may have made reservations at a nearby hotel. I texted Dee about the staying arrangements. I received a text back stating they'd made reservations at one of the hotels near the house—which was what I'd thought.

I knew since her kids liked having a good time with their cousins, they'd most likely stay here.

Trish and I continued talking about what was going on with the rest of the family. Our immediate cousins had sent me gifts to place under the tree for Christmas and cards. Trish and the kids, thankfully, had gotten around to decorating everything before I arrived. It was so pretty around Christmas time, but it was a lot of work putting up and taking down decorations. Trish looked at me and asked what was on my mind.

"I'm fine. No, seriously, just you guys being here is more than I could ask for. I just wish I wasn't estranged for so long. Trish, Christian would not let me leave the house to visit at all. I felt like a prisoner in my own home."

Looking directly at me, Trish put my hands in hers and reassured me that she and all of the family understood the position Christian had put me in.

"We know that was not you doing that, Toni. We always knew he was the deciding factor because you were calling less and less. So we knew what he was up to and trying to do. But as they say, look at God. When I told you the family was praying for you to wake up and leave him, we were PRAYING."

I just sat there and nodded, but I still felt guilty because I'd missed so much time with the kids, with how life was going between everyone. It just wasn't a good feeling to miss out and then feel helpless that you were in a position where you couldn't leave.

"Well, I'm back in you guys' life, and nothing will keep me from it this time. No matter what."

We talked a few minutes more before realizing it was getting late into the night, and I had some preparation to do the next morning, and they had to go to the airport. We both said goodnight and went upstairs to the bedrooms. Waking up the next morning, I felt as if a weight of guilt had been removed. I'd enjoyed our conversation last night and was glad no one was upset with me for being gone from the family for so long. I couldn't believe I'd thought they would be mad at me for something they knew was beyond my control. I got up quickly, took a shower, and threw on some clothes.

Walking downstairs, I heard giggling sounds coming from the living room.

"Good morning, girls," I said, excited to get a start on the day.

"Good morning, Auntie," the girls replied in unison. My siblings and I could never get that unison voice because Dee was always clowning around. Timeka, Tasha, and Tara were up early, it seemed, looking at the TV and, of course, each on their cell phones texting and scrolling. As I thought back to our childhood, our cell phones weren't nearly that advanced. Texting, yes, but social media—there was only Myspace at the time. So we primarily used the phone for actually calling people. These phones were pretty much computers now.

I looked through the refrigerator, grabbing everything needed to get breakfast started. I knew in a few hours Trish and Leon were leaving to pick up Mom and Dad, but I wasn't sure if the girls were riding with them. While in the refrigerator, I grabbed the ham, turkey, and greens and placed them in their pans on the counter. I ended up making breakfast burritos and called the girls into the kitchen. Just then, Leon appeared behind them.

"Sis, can you make me some coffee?"

"I sure can, sir." I turned around and put the coffee pod

into the machine and set another pod to the side for me. The girls grabbed the breakfast burritos and sat down. Leon also grabbed one and waited by the counter for the coffee to finish. He informed me Trish was on her way down too. I thanked my assistant in my mind again that she'd made sure we had all we needed for food. I'd made more than enough breakfast burritos and sat down myself to eat.

Trish came in, whizzing by, and commented that the food smelled good.

"Yes, you guys will need nourishment, especially after you walk to where you have to meet Mom and Dad." I knew that airport too well, and let's just say it was a strong second as one of the biggest airports besides Atlanta.

"Yeah, we definitely had a feel for the walking when we landed here ourselves," Trish replied. The girls said they were going with them to meet their grandparents, so that left me to clean up the kitchen after breakfast and start on the pies I was tasked to make. I said goodbye to each as they headed out the door to get Mom and Dad.

Well, I thought to myself, time to get this kitchen cleaned up and right for Mother. Giggling out loud, I knew how much Mom disliked being called Mother. It was too formal, she said, and when Leon did it, she'd scolded him real quick. Leon had met them years ago when Trish and he first met. He'd asked Dad for permission to marry Trish. I never took Leon seriously until he did that. He gained my respect and became a friend anytime he needed to talk. Thinking back, Christian was jealous, if you can believe it, of the relationship I had with Leon. He would say what grown man needed to tell a woman he wasn't married to his problems. He didn't understand that I also reached out to Leon whenever Christian stressed me out. Leon knew I understood Trish better than anyone because who knows a person better than the sibling they grew up with. I knew her dreams even when she would dismiss them. Leon and I had a lot in common, and I knew deep down he really cared for Trish. Would give her the moon if he could.

Yes, they'd had rough patches in their marriage—all marriages did. It was how you recovered from that patch, though, to keep fighting to be together. After I washed the dishes from breakfast, I went into the living room to get my cell phone off the table. I had several text messages. A few from Dee stating that Tim was able to leave earlier than planned and they'd be in earlier than originally thought. One from our youngest, Kevin, stating he'd be driving in and would be over to visit tomorrow. He added that he was able to bring his son and they'd be staying in a hotel near me. Of course, the last one was from Paul, telling me he'd like to see me within the next couple of months and to let him know my schedule. I also went into my phone and decided to start a dating profile on one of the sites.

Walking back into the kitchen, I cleaned the counters off and then took out the pie crust so it could thaw. The cell started chiming as soon as I took out the ingredients for the pies. "Hello," I said. It was Natalie. "Hey, happy pre-Thanksgiving, Nat." Natalie asked how everything was going and if everyone had arrived yet. "No, Kevin, Dee, and Tim will be in tomorrow. Well, actually, Kevin and his son will be in late tonight but will come over tomorrow. Dee and Tim will be in tomorrow morning, earlier than they were supposed to, thankfully." I told Natalie that Paul had been texting me asking for an update. She laughed back and insisted that I see that man in the next few months. I knew I didn't have a lot going on work-wise, so what was holding me back? Fear. Anxiety. Both of those were deadly combinations to the mind. She shot back into the phone that I needed to take a chance and not miss out because of what I'd just gone through. In my heart of hearts, I knew that, but I had to tell that to my mind. "I am going to, Natalie. I'm just trying to be cautious." She said into the phone, "Okay, I understand that because you're scared to put yourself back out there again. But if you don't, out of fear, you wouldn't know what could have been." She had a valid point on that.

As we said our goodbyes, I turned back to mixing up the sweet potato pie ingredients together. Then I walked over to the stove, turning it on so that by the time I finished mixing and pouring into the pie crusts, the oven would be ready for baking them. Hearing my phone chime again, I looked at the text message from Trish. "Still waiting on Mom and Dad to arrive." I texted back okay and finished up pouring the mix into both of the pie crusts. After putting both pies into the oven and setting the timer, I grabbed the items needed for the turkey and started on those. Mom always cooked the turkey, and if I wasn't mistaken, she'd shown Trish how to make the turkey but asked that she do it only after Mom had passed on. I thought to myself that was ridiculous, but it was what Mom wanted.

As I was finishing up what could be prepared ahead of Mom and Dad's arrival, Trish texted me about an hour or so later stating they had Mom and Dad and were on the way back to the house. At that time, I vacuumed the living room and cut up the ingredients for the ham, turkey, and turkey wings. I washed the greens down, then let them soak. I finally was able to sit down and look at what was on the television. Hearing the doorbell, I knew Mom and Dad were here, and I became excited. It had been more than a few years since I'd seen them as well.

"Hey, Mom. Hey, Dad," I said at the door while moving out of the way so they could walk in.

"Hey, love," Dad said and instantly grabbed a hug from me. It felt so good to hug him again that I almost cried, but I didn't want to make it a thing. Then Mom walked in and hugged me too, nice and tight.

"Baby girl, we missed you so much," she said, giving me a kiss on the cheek. "You have lost so much weight. Are you eating?" she said with a concern in her voice.

The rest of the clan walked back into the living room, and the girls went upstairs to look at the television. Trish and Leon went into the kitchen to start on the rest of the food and left me alone with Mom and Dad. They knew there was nothing like talking face-to-face with family you hadn't seen in a long time. I motioned for both of them to sit on the sofa while I began to unpack the last several years.

"Well, as you know, it's official that I'm no longer in the marriage," I continued. "I want to apologize for not having been around for so long and that I literally had to escape if I wanted to fly back and see you guys." They both nodded that they understood and that no apology was needed. "I was only allowed to contact you both if Christian was at home, and that was hardly ever, especially in the last three years."

They both hugged me again, and Dad said he knew what was happening but felt so helpless not being able to stop it. Mom asked again about the weight, and I had to reassure her that I was eating fine and that the stress of the divorce had made me a thinner person. Honestly, being smaller than I was gave me a reason to revamp my eating habits. I was always a snacker, for better or for worse. The weight loss, to me, looked better on me. I knew my parents were always used to seeing a curvy me, but I liked the smaller curves I had now.

Focusing back to Mom and Dad, I told them both I missed them and would promise to visit often to make up for lost time. Mom stood up and proceeded to go into the kitchen. Leon came back into the living room and sat down with us. He knew, as much as Trish did, that I needed that alone time with my parents for my mental saneness. The few times I did see the family, I'd always wondered why Leon couldn't stand Christian, and with the recent revelation, I now knew why. Most of the family couldn't stand Christian, and him alienating me had made the hate that much worse. Christian knew deep down they only tolerated him for my sake, and in his mind, he took pleasure in that.

Leon and Tim knew I was not the same person Christian had married, and I knew it made them both angry that my light had dimmed out and my confidence had faded. I'd become someone who was a stranger to the family. Leon, being around me now, realized the old me was slowly coming back. Before, on the rare visits, Dee and Trish were really the only two who would talk to me, but even then, they knew I'd changed and this person they didn't even recognize. I was paranoid and would avoid eye contact and constantly look for Christian to be nearby. The other times, I'd be zoned out mentally. I didn't want them to keep seeing me like that. Christian would fill my head with all the lies that he said they said behind my back.

I shook my head and thought how naïve I was when

I walked into the marriage. Christian would only share what he thought I wanted to hear and would do and say all of the right things. Then he would come back and throw them in my face later. He was a master manipulator, and one of his past girlfriends tried to warn me. I was too headstrong, thinking she was delusional. Christian told me she had mental problems and was constantly lying. Almost everyone in the family but me saw what Christian was. Oh, they tried at first to talk me into leaving him, especially Leon. Leon had a few ex-friends that were just like Christian.

In college, Leon had a former teammate who was just like Christian and would often ask me if Christian had any siblings. He did, but not any brothers. Anyway, the teammate would often tell Leon that he needed help with his course-work because Leon maintained a decent GPA in college. Then he would go to him to borrow money because he knew Leon's parents were financially stable. After several months of this happening, Leon became hip to the game, so to speak, and cut him off cold. He told him their friendship was over and not to do anything but focus on playing football.

The guy then had a mental meltdown in front of the whole team one night after practice, telling everyone Leon was asking him to do his coursework for him. Leon almost got kicked off the team and out of school if it wasn't for the proof he had of every time that guy asked him for money. He literally showed the coach and dean every time money was sent to his account and put into that guy's account. Needless to say, after that, Leon was cautious about making friends with anyone. I couldn't blame him one bit.

Then when my situation came along, Leon even stated he would find me one of his single friends and set me up with them. He told me from the start Christian was bad news. "Toni, I know his type. I've been around them at college, and they become worse with money. You don't have to rush into this marriage just to appease his parents. He will use you as a trophy or a toy and then drain you mentally, emotionally, and physically. Don't do this. I have a few friends that are single, and they know of you. They really want to take you out." Leon tried desperately to talk me out of getting married over the phone one night. "Leon, I like him, and I know I can love him," I'd said back stupidly.

Even after all of that, Leon still supported my decision and said he would watch from a distance, but he knew how this would turn out. If only my heart and mind could've seen how much of a downward spiral this would go. I still couldn't help but blame myself for everything that went on. Snapping out of my thoughts, I went into the kitchen to join Trish and Mom in cooking. I hadn't even realized the pies had finished, but Trish had taken them out of the oven. "It's okay, Toni. They were done, and I know you were bonding with Dad out there." "Thanks, Trish."

Mom was putting the turkey into the cooking pan after thoroughly cleaning it out. Trish was putting the greens on the stove after rinsing them and removing dirt from them. I started on the stuffing, and Mom started humming as she was fixing the turkey to prep it for the oven. Her humming brought back so many memories of when I was a kid. There wasn't too much talking going on in the kitchen—we were just happy to be in each other's company. "Okay, everything is moving along smoothly. Have you two spoken to Dee and Tim?" Mom inquired. "Yeah," me and Trish said in unison. "She and Tim are coming in on Thanksgiving morning.

They're getting on the plane late tonight to get here early tomorrow," Trish concluded.

"Okay, good, because I want to talk to Dee and catch up on her kids' lives." I turned around and looked at Mom. "Wait, she hasn't been speaking to you lately?" Concern had crept into my question. "No, not really. I may hear from her once a month now." Even Trish was shocked by this. "Wait, she told me that she had just talked to you last week," Trish said, now looking concerned. "No, I hadn't spoken to her for three weeks," Mom stated while shaking her head. "Okay, now what is going on?" I wondered. Why was Dee lying about when she spoke to Mom, and for what reason? It was strange to lie about something so small as talking with someone.

"Something isn't right then," Trish continued. "Now, I didn't say that to start any trouble between you three. It had to be something she didn't want to really reveal if she lied to you two about when we spoke last." Well, that didn't exactly make me feel at peace. If anything, I had more questions to ask Dee when she got here. Trish and I would have a heart-to-heart conversation with her, but I had to tell Trish that if we did, we couldn't interrogate her as if we were the police.

"So are they driving from the airport tomorrow, or will one of you be picking them up?" Mom asked. "She told me they were renting a car and driving because they'll also be staying at the same hotel that Kevin will be at," I said, looking at Mom. "Before you ask, Kevin is coming in this evening. He's supposed to text me when he gets in," I told Mom. "Okay, good, even though I see Kevin more often than I even see Dee," Mom stated. "I even see the Trish family more than I've seen Dee within these last few years." This time I was the one in shock. It wasn't like Dee not to pick up the phone or visit on a regular basis. "I'm just concerned about her in these last few years, that's all," Mom said.

Rightfully so, Mom was to be concerned. I was concerned about the lying part, not the visitation. Mom had to get used to me not visiting or calling, and I was sure that wasn't easy on her peace of mind. She hasn't said that, but I knew that was how she felt. Dee, on the other hand, was consistent on a regular basis. If she didn't visit at least three times a year, she would call Mom and Dad almost every day. So to go from that to hardly talking but once a month—something was up. Now I couldn't wait to see her and Tim tomorrow and ask what the deal was.

Several hours later, Mom asked for both Trish and me to help her remove the turkey from the oven.

"Oh man, that smells so good," Trish remarked.

I agreed. "Mom put her foot in that turkey," I giggled.

Mom looked at both of us with wide eyes and a smile on her face. "I can't believe tomorrow is Thanksgiving."

I was shaking my head at how fast the year flew by.

"Right," Trish started, interrupting my thoughts. "It seemed only yesterday that it was summertime."

Mom agreed this time. "I'm just glad I'm with you guys, especially Toni."

I smiled and walked back into the living room to check out what was playing on the television.

Trish came a few minutes later to join me. Mom finished basting the turkey with the juices so it could be tender for tomorrow and asked one of us to help her place it back in the oven. I decided to go and help since I had to take out the stuffing. Mom told me thank you, and I removed the stuffing from the oven and placed it on the counter. "I think

I'm going to make bread pudding," Mom said and began to go into the refrigerator and the cabinets to take out the ingredients. "Oh yeah, Mom, that's a good idea," I nodded. I mean, the pies were there, but the bread pudding was like the icing on the cake. It added additional options for those who didn't want pie. Mom made hers with the icing on top, and it was so delicious.

"Oh, I don't know if I have raisins, though, Mom," I said as I was helping her look in the pantry.

"Do you mind going to the store and getting them?" she asked, knowing I would not say no.

"Sure, I'll be right back." As I walked into the living room area, Trish had heard that part of the conversation and asked if she could join me. I nodded for her to come along, and we both went outside and got into the car.

As soon as the car started, the phone rang. It was Kevin letting me know they'd landed and were heading to the hotel to rest before coming over in the morning. He was on the Bluetooth speaker in the car, and Trish said hi.

"Hey, sis, how have you been?" Kevin questioned.

"I've been doing well, Kevin." They continued to small talk some more, and then we both said I love you to him and hung up the phone.

"Kevin hasn't been to a family gathering in what seems like forever, right?" Trish asked.

"Yeah, almost as long as I have," I agreed back.

Arriving at the store, Trish stayed in the car while I ran in to get some raisins and heavy whipping cream for the icing to go on the bread pudding. Several minutes later, I opened the door and got back into the car.

"Girl, so what do you think of these lies Dee has been

telling us?" Trish asked curiously.

"I don't know, but I know I want to ask her as soon as she gets in tomorrow," I agreed back. At this point, inquiring minds wanted to know who or what she was covering for.

"I wonder if it's something that she and Tim are going through in their marriage and she doesn't want anyone to know," I pointed out.

Trish shook her head. "I don't know, but we have to get to the bottom and figure out if Dee is in danger or in an abusive situation or what."

We both thought the worst considering the situation I'd just barely escaped from. It really pained me to think that Dee was in a similar situation and she'd helped me when she was going through the same thing.

"Hopefully, we'll get the answers tomorrow when she comes in," I said with slight optimism.

Reaching the house, we both got out of the car and walked in.

"Mom, here are the items you needed," I said. Trish went upstairs to see what the girls and Leon were up to. I informed Mom that Kevin had called and said he and Donte were tired from the flight and would join us in the morning. I grabbed the stuffing and placed it in the fridge along with the greens and pies. The turkey was still cooking and wouldn't be finished until late or early in the morning. I kissed Mom goodnight, and Dad, I noticed, had already gone up to bed. Mom said he had a bit of jet lag and turned in early. I left the television on for Mom since she'd be up for the turkey to finish cooking.

Arriving upstairs, Trish was still watching television,

and Leon had fallen asleep on her. She said goodnight and that the kids had already gone to sleep. I went toward my bedroom, and once inside, I decided to take a shower before bed.

After jumping out of the shower, I dried off and put some moisturizer on my skin. I noticed my phone had a few notifications on it. Looking at the phone, most were from the dating profile site I'd subscribed to. I replied back to a few interested gentlemen but took the interest as just that. Online dating used to be so crazy, and it had been a long time for me. Half of the decent profiles were scammers. The other half were people with old pictures who hadn't looked that way in years. A very slim few were actual people who were legit. I slid into the bed and dozed off into dreamland.

4

POISONED TRUTHS

Waking up to birds chirping, I took a quick wash in the sink and then got dressed to go downstairs and greet Kevin, Dee, and Tim. Looking at my phone, Kevin had texted me early and said he was on his way over. As I exited the bedroom, I noticed that Trish and Leon weren't up yet, and neither were the girls. Walking down the stairs, I noticed that Mom and Dad were both up, and I could smell the aroma of coffee coming from the kitchen. Both were sitting at the kitchen table drinking when I went over to them and hugged them.

"Good morning," I said.

"Good morning," they said back, almost in unison. I went over to the coffee machine and put a pod in to make some for myself as well.

"The coffee is smelling good this morning."

"Yes, I made me and my lovebug some," Mom said.

I loved it when she used pet names for Dad. Their bond was nearly unbreakable.

"Yeah, I see. I could smell that coffee from the stairs," I said teasingly but only half-joking.

Just then, the doorbell rang. I started to walk in that direction, but Dad motioned me to stay, and he answered the door instead.

"Hey, Dad. Hey, Grandpa," Kevin and his son said.

"Well, finally I get to see my grandson. It's been too long, Kevin," Dad stated.

"I know, Dad. I'm having to work through my schedule. It's been hectic the last few years," he shot back as he hugged him.

"Grandpa, can we play catch outside?" Donte asked.

"Wait, you have to meet the rest of the family first, son," Kevin interrupted him.

Just then, I walked into the living room and saw Kevin for the first time in more than eight years. He looked much older and still had that charismatic smile on him.

"Heyyyyy, Toni," he said, staring at me.

"Hey, lil bro. I'm glad you could make it and bring out Donte since I haven't seen him since he was a baby," I said.

Just then, Trish and Leon walked down the stairs together and spoke to Kevin. I went over to where Kevin was and gave him a much-needed hug. We didn't talk like we used to, and I didn't want to make it awkward.

"Oh man, I missed your hugs, sis," he said, and then Trish interjected.

"Hey, what about my hugs?"

"Yeah, I know, but I hug you on the regular. It's been too long since I've seen Toni. I know it wasn't your fault, Toni.

I understand what you were going through, and I have no ill feelings toward what happened. I just want you to know that," he said with a sincere tone. It made me feel really good that he didn't blame me for the way Christian would act.

"Okay, Grandpa, can we go outside now?" Donte asked again.

"Yes, young man, we can go out now," Dad replied and escorted Donte outside.

Kevin asked, "So when are Dee and Tim getting here?"

"Supposedly this morning, but I have yet to hear from them," Trish said, then looked at me.

"Yeah, they haven't texted me either," I added. Looking confused, Kevin shook his head and tried to call Dee himself. Surprise—no answer.

"It's still early. Maybe they're in mid-flight now and unable to turn on the cell phone yet," I assured him and Trish.

Kevin had been known to get into protection mode when it concerned the rest of the siblings. He definitely didn't take any mess when it came to Tim or Christian. Leon and he got along right from the start. They were both into games and both loved computers. Leon had said he would've been a computer programmer, but the patience that was needed it was better he be a doctor. Christian had gotten on Kevin's bad side in the past, and it turned ugly. This played into why my ex-husband wouldn't want me to come and visit them without him being present. That way, they couldn't talk me into staying with one of them and filing for divorce without him dragging it out. However, a great lawyer and friend was introduced to me, and the rest, as they say, was history.

"I hope that is the case," Kevin shot a look at both of us that we both recognized. "Now, bro, don't go off on the deep end. It's not that serious to be concerned yet," Trish said and gave him a hug, trying to calm him down. All three of us sat down on the sofa and checked out what Mom was looking at on the television.

Leon had gone into the kitchen to fix something to eat and asked if we wanted anything.

"I'm so glad you're home, son," Mom said with loving eyes. "Me too, Mom," he agreed back.

Dad opened the door, and he and Donte walked in. "Thank you, Grandpa," Donte said as he walked toward the living room. Donte walked in front of us until he got to Mom.

"Hi, Grandma," he said. She instantly hugged and kissed his cheeks. "You're getting tall like your father."

"Yes, ma'am, I know." Then he ran upstairs to see what the girls were up to. I shook my head watching him run up the stairs. Mom was right—he was almost taking those stairs two at a time with his long legs.

"That son of mine is growing so fast. As soon as I think I'm done buying shoes, his feet grow two more inches," Kevin said as he chuckled.

"Mom and Dad, thank you for always giving us what we needed during those growing years, especially me," Kevin said as he looked lovingly at both parents.

"Son, we thought we had to take out a second mortgage on the house just for your basketball shoes," Dad jokingly shot back, not missing a beat. We all laughed at that one in unison. I remembered when Dad would ask Kevin what he was eating differently to cause his feet to grow so fast. We knew early in our teens that Kevin was going to be taller than all of us.

Just then my phone rang, I picked it up and put it on speaker.

"Hey, Toni, we just landed," Dee said. "Okay, good. We were wondering if we had to send a search party to the airport, Dee," I shook my head and shot back into the phone.

"No, nothing like that. We ran into some turbulence and had to fly through a storm, so we couldn't have our cell phones on," she stated.

"Everyone is here and waiting on you two to get here so we can talk," I said, hoping to get some answers to where the lies were coming from.

"I know. We're picking up the luggage now and heading to the rental car area to pick up the car."

"The kids are here and can't wait to see their older cousins and the baby cousin." She assured me they'd text when they pulled up in front of the house.

"Okay, take care and be safe driving here," I said and hung up the phone.

"Okay, it looks like everyone will be here together after all," Mom said. Trish and I couldn't wait to question Dee. Kevin went into the kitchen to talk with Leon. Mom and Dad also got up and went into the kitchen to make sure everything was ready or at least heated up to eat for later on. Trish and I sat on the couch and just enjoyed some small talk while we watched another Christmas movie. In one of the bedrooms, I'd purchased a game system so the kids could have something to do while they were here. I knew with all this technology, they weren't the going outside type like we were. We would split our time between outside activities and games and social media.

Around an hour later, I got the text from Dee that they were out front.

"She's here," I said to Trish, and both of us met them at the door. I opened the main door to the glass door in front of it. As we stood there, we saw them piling out of the car, and I thought to myself why didn't Tim rent an SUV since they would've had more legroom and luggage room. Dee almost sprinted to the front door. Opening the door, I let her and the kids coming behind her in.

"Dee, oh, I missed you," I said as I hugged her tight. Then she went to Trish and gave her a big hug. The kids came in and hugged me so close.

"We missed you, Aunt Toni. Where have you been?" Brad asked with concern. "

I'm here now, and that's the most important part," I said, trying to reassure him. I gave them a good long hug and told them I wasn't going anywhere anymore. Then they shot up the stairs looking for where the other cousins were.

In one of their hands, I noticed they had a Nintendo Switch. I thought that was good since the last thing I wanted was for them to be fighting over the games. Brad was the oldest and looked just like Tim. He was a mocha complexion with a short haircut known as a Caesar cut. Then Brittani was a classic middle child. Her hair was in short locs, and her red-bone freckled face was nice, full, and round. She and I were almost the same height. Her mannerisms were after her mom, though. She was a little younger than Timeka but just as smart and fierce. She loved the attention and often rubbed it in her cousins' faces. All of Dee's kids had grown a lot since I'd last laid eyes on them.

The youngest was Curt. He was definitely the baby for a while until Donte came along. We spoiled Curt rotten, and he knew it. He never competed, though, for attention from Donte. He thought of himself as a big brother to Donte. He often would tell Donte how to sneak candy. Curt was a bit on the chunky side, but he'd lost all of that weight when Dee told me he was playing soccer. He was really skinny now with big brown eyes and a head full of curls. He, I must say, got the best of both Dee and Tim in the genes department. I could see him being like Kevin, a heartbreaker for sure. Thinking back, I remembered when Kevin had to beat the girls off of him. He was tall in middle school, and all the girls wanted to be his girlfriend. We told him middle school was way too young to date a girl. He had more social media growing up than we did, and Mom plus Dad had to monitor his cell phone to make sure there were no creeps trying to talk to him on those chat rooms.

Tim walked into the house, and Trish and I spoke to him. He heard Dad talking from the kitchen with Kevin and decided to head that way. I shook my head and thought that was about to get real interesting. Dee sat on the sofa with Trish and me. Since most of the family were in the kitchen, we looked at her and asked her to follow us upstairs to my bedroom.

"Okay, Dee, what is going on with you lately?" Trish started off immediately.

"What are you talking about now, Trish?" Dee said, looking confused.

"Why have Toni and I found out that you've been lying to us about when you would talk to Mom?"

"You told us that you talked with Mom just last week and two weeks before that," she continued. "Then Mom is telling us you haven't spoken to her in at least a month."

Dee looked around, all of a sudden nervous. I noticed the immediate shift in her demeanor because I'd had that a few times throughout my marriage.

"Okay, please don't judge me, you guys, and please do not say anything about this to Tim," Dee began.

"I am miserable in my marriage to Tim," she continued. "I got bored, and I felt like I was just here to bear kids, and my life just became so routine. Between the kids' sports and Tim's work schedule, I just don't know how much longer I can do this."

Trish interrupted, "Listen, we both understand where you're coming from."

I added to the conversation, "Look, I know how it is. Christian was trying to control anyone and everyone around me, and I got tired and didn't know how to dig out of the rut and control he had over me," I continued. "I had sunk so low that my self-esteem took a big hit. I didn't think anyone would want me but him."

"I know, but I started getting on these dating sites and started meeting men to make me feel alive again," Dee said, looking like she was going to cry at any minute.

"I know it was wrong. I wanted someone to make me feel like a woman and want me like I needed to be wanted," she said.

"So what happened?"

"I started seeing this guy, and we started sleeping together." Tears started rolling from her eyes as soon as she said it.

"Trish and Toni, I'm not the perfect sister you guys think I am. I messed up big time," she confessed.

This time, Trish took over the conversation. "I know you aren't perfect. Toni and I never thought that. You're human, and like you stated, you were just going through the motions and not feeling like you were needed," she nodded in agreement. "The important thing now is where or with whom is your heart?" Trish asked. "What are you going to do at this point?"

Dee replied back, "I don't know what to do. I don't know if I want to try counseling or just call it quits," she said.

"Tim doesn't seem to think we need marriage counseling, but I told him about my feelings, and he said he would think about doing it."

"I'm at my wit's end, and he doesn't seem to care."

I then interrupted, "Well, if he doesn't, you make the appointment and start going by yourself until he joins you. I can't tell you any more than that because you see where I'm at."

Trish then said, "If counseling is the way you're going, you're going to have to end it with the other guy involved. It won't work if you're still seeing the other person. The other guy is just a distraction." She walked over to Dee and gave her a big hug. I then proceeded to do the same. We let her know she wasn't alone, and whatever she decided, she would also have to discuss it with her children.

"You guys don't know how good it felt to finally talk about it," Dee said as she embraced us harder. "I know I'll have to tell the kids and Tim. I think I'll talk to Tim about it while I'm here," she confirmed. "Good," I said while walking over to the bed and taking a seat.

In my mind, I just wished I didn't have my own drama going on so that Dee would have felt comfortable coming to me before the situation got to this point. I did slightly look up to her and Tim's marriage and wished my marriage to Christian was more like theirs. Now I realized none of their marriages were perfect, and what I thought was good wasn't.

"Dee, I just want you to know if you need to talk after you tell Tim what happened, I'm here," I reaffirmed to her. She needed to know I had her back, and no matter what I had going on, I'd be there—unlike before.

"I know, Toni, and I appreciate it. Just you listening and understanding that I was in a bad place when I decided to find someone else outside of the marriage," she started with sorrow in her eyes. "Tim gets so into his work that he forgets there's another partner to consider. I never meant to hurt him, but at the same time, I felt alone, and I tried so many times to talk to him. He wouldn't listen and thought I was being overly dramatic." She had a familiar sound of frustration in her voice. I was all too familiar with that sound of giving up and just going with the flow.

A hard knock at the door jolted all of us out of the conversation. "Yes," I answered. "Hey, you guys okay in there?" It was Dad. We collectively breathed a sigh of relief. The last thing we wanted was for Tim to be at that door wanting an explanation of why we were talking amongst ourselves.

"Yes, Dad, we'll be out in a minute," I replied. "Okay," he answered back and started walking back down the stairs. The kids had been so wrapped up in the game they were playing that they hadn't even noticed we were in the bedroom talking. Which, with the turn of events, was a good thing.

All three of us walked down the stairs when Timeka asked what time we were eating.

"Well, as soon as Dee finishes up her dish," Trish

replied. It brought back old memories of all three of us walking down the stairs. I remembered when I was going to prom, and Dee and Trish walked me down the stairs to see my date. Lonnie was his name. Lonnie was tall, about six-three and darker complexion, with a beautiful Caesar haircut and those forever deep waves. He continuously brushed his hair to ensure his waves were one of the best-looking in school. He was captain of the football team and knew he was committing to a D1 school. He treated me so well, and I felt bad that I'd already been accepted at Texas A&M. We left each other on good terms, and years later, I saw him on television playing for the Philadelphia Eagles.

Snapping out of that thought, I walked into the kitchen with Trish and Dee and started putting the food in the oven to warm everything up. As Dee was finishing up her dish, Tim walked into the kitchen asking if any of us needed help. We all nodded that we didn't. Then Dee asked her husband if they could go in the other room so they could talk. I wasn't sure what the reaction from Tim would be, but I just hoped they'd reach an understanding and begin to repair their marriage. While most of the food was warming up, I started setting up the trays that would hold the food. We often would set up the food like a buffet so everyone could get what they wanted.

Dee and Tim walked back to where we were, and Tim looked upset, to say the least. "Toni, I'll be back. I have to leave and get some air," he said and walked toward the door. After he left the house, Trish and I looked at Dee, waiting for her to spill his reaction to what she'd told him.

"Well, he didn't take the news well at all. I told him we need to go to counseling because I feel like I'm wanting to file for divorce," she said, and I saw the tears in her eyes again. "He said okay, we'll seek counseling because he doesn't feel like we need a divorce," she continued. "He started to cry a little when I told him about the cheating. He said he felt hurt and betrayed and that I should've come to him first. I then told him I tried several times and that he ignored me or didn't want to talk. Then he was like, 'This is my fault that you decided to cheat.' I told him it's both of our faults and that he gets so wrapped up in a case that he just ignores everything else going on in life, including me. He said he understood and would try to do better," Dee explained.

"Well, all you can do is try and get everything out in the open during counseling," Trish stated. "He left to clear his head, Dee, because that was a lot that you told him," I interjected.

"I know," she said, turning to the oven and checking on the ham.

"Please keep us posted on whatever you guys decide," I said and started putting the food into the trays. The only thing we were waiting on was the ham to finish cooking. We had sweet potato pies, potato salad, greens, turkey, stuffing, rolls, deviled eggs, and ham. That was more than enough for all of us. Most of the family didn't like candied yams, so I left that off of my to-do list. Trish made the gravy option for those who liked turkey and gravy. I didn't care for gravy since the turkey already put folks to sleep—otherwise known as a food coma.

About an hour later, Tim came back into the house, and I noticed Dad had gone with him. Maybe Dad was the reasoning in case Tim was thinking of doing something to himself. That news to some men could crush their ego or cause them to doubt themselves and everything they believed. Deep down, I was glad Dad had gone with Tim. I heard a knock on the door and noticed Mom went to answer it this time. Hugging Kevin and his son, they both walked in and dropped down on the sofa. The Thanksgiving football game was playing on the television. The cousins who were upstairs were starting to come down due to smelling the aroma of food throughout the house, which was good because that meant I didn't have to yell for anyone to come down.

The trays were lined up on the kitchen counter, and the ham finally was finished. Everyone started piling into the kitchen, and Dad started saying grace over the food. It definitely was a spread. I missed these moments and realized I was still loved. I was still able to pick up the pieces of my life and put them back together. I was in no hurry to date but also realized I wasn't getting any younger to have children. After the grace was said, everyone went around the table and stated what they were thankful for. When it came to me, I said I was thankful for finding family and love again. It was the truth. My family had come through and were supporting me where I needed support. I was so appreciative of that, and they had no idea what impact that had on me.

"Okay, line up and dig in," Mom said with so much love in her voice. I saw genuine happiness in her and Dad's faces. I decided to grab what I wanted and sit in the living room and eat. Trish and Dee joined me along with Dad and Kevin. I'd bought some TV trays shortly after I moved in and brought them out for this occasion. As we were sitting around watching the football game, Dee and Dad started talking about the situation that had transpired. Dee was learning from Dad while they were talking. I was glad we had that type of relationship with Dad where we could tell him almost anything. Almost anything... Dad didn't want to know about our relations with our husbands or any feminine issues going on with us. I laughed to myself. I remembered a few times in the household when Dee and Trish wanted to tell Dad how they hated that time of the month; the woman curse, Auntie Flo visiting, that monthly pain. We had all sorts of nicknames for that time of the month. Dad was not hearing any of that. He would often step out of the room if we brought it up around him.

Dad's parents, especially Dwayne, his father, often told him not to be in the room when women brought up the cramping they went through. That's what their mom was for, to handle those conversations. As a man, we have no clue what type of pain they go through. Shaking my head, I smiled, remembering Dad telling us that Grandpa would leave the room as well. Grandpa Dwayne passed away several years ago, and I didn't even go to the funeral. I just wanted to remember how he was before he got sick. That, I thought, was going to break Dad because he and his dad were real close. Sofia, Dad's mom, had passed away while Dee and I were in high school. All of us went to her funeral, but as teens, Dee and I didn't understand how her death would change our lives.

Focusing back on the football game, Kevin got up and went into the kitchen for seconds. I shook my head at how he was able to put away so much food. Had to be the long torso—more stomach room. I was full and took my plate to the kitchen. Trish was done as well, so I grabbed hers. Leon came out of the kitchen asking if his wife needed any more food.

"No, I'm good, baby," she said. Leon went in for seconds as well. I noticed Dad and Dee still talking, so I decided to give them some time alone and talk to Kevin and his son in the kitchen.

"So how are you guys doing?" I asked, looking at both my brother and his twin.

"I'm ready for school to start again, Auntie Toni. I like playing soccer with the team, and I miss not being able to practice," Donte stated with excitement in his voice.

"That's good, little man," I said, continuing, "I'm glad you love soccer so much. Are you going to play professionally?"

"Yes, I want to," he agreed. "We'll see soon because you still have to get through middle and high school while playing soccer to see if that's something you want to do professionally," Kevin cosigned.

"You say that now because you love being on the team, but having to play all throughout the next six years, you may change your mind and not like it as much," Kevin added.

"No, Dad, I don't see that happening," his son interrupted.

"Okay, we'll see you in high school if you still feel the same," I reassured him.

Just then, Brittani and Curt asked to be excused to go upstairs and play on the game system. They'd pretty much finished their food, and I nodded and gathered the plates into the kitchen sink. I was definitely going to use the dishwasher. I think I'd used it when I first moved in just to ensure it was working with no issues, and that was it. It was just me in this house, so I figured handwashing a few dishes was fine. My other nieces and nephew were still engaging Kevin in conversation since they rarely got to see him. All I heard was giggling and laughing as Kevin attempted to say a few jokes in between the conversation. I left some of the food out in the trays and began to wrap up the leftovers and place them in the refrigerator. Kevin stopped his conversation and went over to help me.

"I think I'll make Donte and me a plate and head back to the hotel for a bit," Kevin said, then continued, "They have a pool, and I know Donte wanted to get in it before it got too dark. I do too, truth be told."

"Okay, I hear ya. Make sure to ask the others if they want to go to the pool with you and take them," I added.

"Okay, let me ask them now," he said back. Kevin turned to our nieces and nephew and asked if they wanted to go back with him to the hotel to get in the pool there. Brad and Tara both said yes. Timeka and Tasha said no. "I don't want to get my locs wet. It takes way too long to dry," Timeka replied. Kevin nodded in agreement and went upstairs to ask the rest of the kids. Kevin had a nice-size truck he'd rented, so he had extra space. Coming down the stairs were his son, Curt, and Brittani. They all decided to go and came up to me and gave hugs. I told them I'd see them in the morning. Trish emerged from the living area and asked Tara if she'd packed her swimsuit. She nodded and said she'd packed a small bag with some overnight clothes in it. She asked Dee's kids if they'd brought any clothes with them, and they nodded they had. Curt went to where Dee was and asked for the car keys. He told his mom he was going to stay at the hotel with Kevin and Donte. She nodded, and he proceeded to go to the car to get his clothes together, and Brittani followed suit.

"Kevin," Trish asked, "is your room big enough for all these kids?"

"Yes, I booked a suite, and it has a pull-out sofa for the kids," he responded. Kevin had his own bed, and his son had his own bed. The beds were queen-size, so his cousins Brad and Curt could sleep there, while Brittani and Tara could sleep on the pull-out. Kevin said his goodbyes and that he'd drop the kids back off in the morning. Everyone waved at them as they left out the door. I stood watch at the window as I saw them pile into the big truck with bags in tow. Kevin looked like a kid, and it was evident as he handled them with ease. He never stated why his relationship never worked out with his kid's mom. Then again, I wasn't as close with him as I should've been. Trish knew the story, but she hadn't shared it with me or Dee.

By the time the kids were leaving, Dee and Dad had finished up their conversation, and Dee motioned for me to follow her into the kitchen. Trish was in the kitchen already after kissing Tara goodbye. "I feel better about getting counseling after I talked with Dad," Dee said with a smile on her face. "He told me that Tim had a long conversation with him about how he regretted taking on more work at the office and that he could enlist one of the partners to take some of his workload over," she said, then continued, "Tim told Dad he knew it had gotten bad but not bad to where his wife needed to entertain another man." "Dad had told him it wasn't about the other man—it was the lack of attention that Tim was giving in the relationship that the other man was," I nodded in agreement. Dad was often a wise man beyond his years, and through experience, he was able to talk to Tim. "Dad also encouraged Tim to reach out to his parents and tell them what's been happening," Dee stated. "That's actually a good idea," Trish nodded.

I appreciated all of the advice I'd ever received from our father. We sat around and talked for some more and realized the time had slipped by and it was getting late. Trish decided to head upstairs to one of the spare rooms, and Dee and I were sitting at the table talking some more.

Dee asked if she could stay over. She didn't feel like Tim was in a good headspace to be around her at the hotel without the kids there.

"Sure, you know that's a given, girl," I said. She thanked me and told me she'd crash in my room with me. I told her where the towels and washcloths were, and she walked out of the room. Even until we were teens, Dee and I always shared a room. Our parents felt that since we were closer in age, we were able to without too much tension in the room. Trish and Dee, on the other hand—those two were like oil and water growing up. Trish, being the oldest, tried to boss everyone around when she was a teenager. Well, our parents weren't having none of that and sat her down one day to get her straight. After that, she pretty much sat back and let us do whatever.

Getting up from the table, I started cleaning the kitchen and loading up the dishwasher. Mom and Dad had both gone upstairs, I noticed as I peeked from the kitchen into the living room. I finished up in the kitchen and headed upstairs myself to get into bed. I went into the bedroom, seeing Dee already asleep and snoring a bit. At least she isn't loud, I thought to myself. Sliding into the king-size bed, I had more than enough room between Dee and me.

"Sweet dreams, sis," I whispered.

5

COFFEE AND CONFESSIONS

The next morning was Black Friday—the infamous shopaholic day after Thanksgiving. Waking up, I turned to see if Dee was still asleep, but she wasn't even there. Probably getting coffee, I thought to myself. I jumped into the shower, got dressed, and headed downstairs to hear several conversations going on in the kitchen. Dad and Mom were both up and, of course, making coffee for the rest of the family. Most of the family were coffee consumers. I grabbed a cup out of the cabinet after saying good morning to everyone. Pretty much everyone was in the kitchen except for the kids who didn't go with Kevin the night before.

"Kevin texted and said he would be here in another hour to drop off the kids and say his goodbyes to us," Trish stated. I nodded in acknowledgment and sat down to join in the conversation at the table. Dad and Leon were talking about the game last night. Apparently, Dad's team lost despite the newscasters predicting different results. Tim still hadn't called Dee or anyone else for that matter. Dee and Trish were into a deep conversation about planning a trip for Christmas for the family. Mom looked at me as I sat down and said,

"Are you okay, baby? Did you sleep well last night?"

"Yes, Mama, I did sleep well, and I'm okay. Just worried about Dee is all," I said.

We talked about whether we were going to buy anything online for Black Friday. Then some small talk about plans for today and who was leaving and staying.

"When are you going back into the office?" Mom inquired.

"More likely, Mom, after Christmas. I'd like to start the new year with a fresh outlook, especially on work."

Mom nodded and got up to grab some coffee. I turned to the conversation that Dee and Trish were having. Dad and Leon decided to go into the living room and watch television. It had been too long since I'd had people in the house with me. I enjoyed this change and decided to ask Mom if she and Dad would like to stay through Christmas. Mom said she would check with Dad and make sure nothing was needed to attend to at home. A smile spread across my face as I sipped on the hot coffee.

I heard the doorbell ring, but Dad yelled that he would get it. Kevin and the gang of kids came through the door.

"Man, we had so much fun in the pool, you guys," Brad said. All of the kids nodded in unison.

"I got to swim into the deep part," Curt chimed in.

Brittani and Tara had noticeable tans on their skin, and I added,

"Yeah, it definitely looks like the ladies enjoyed the sun a bit too well."

They both looked at me and struck poses as if they were models. I laughed. They were such characters, I thought to myself.

"I'm glad you guys had a good time with each other," Mom said and then asked Kevin what time the flight was.

"We have to get to the airport within the next hour. I really was trying to get here earlier but realized these kids needed nourishment," he replied, looking at the group of kids and at the same time amazed at how smooth last night went. No arguing back and forth, fighting over games, or anything like that—which meant, as a whole, the kids were growing up. The last time he took them all out, let's just say it didn't go as planned, and everything that could go wrong went wrong.

Donte went around giving hugs as his dad said they had to get ready to leave. I really didn't want Kevin to go. That was my little brother, and I missed the talks we used to have when we were younger. I walked them to the car and kissed Donte on the cheek. Immediately, he wiped it off. I shook my head, laughing to myself.

"Bye, lil bro," I said.

"Bye, Toni. I'll text you when we arrive at home."

"Please do," I said, walking back toward the house.

Mom was standing at the door waving as they were backing out of the driveway. Closing the door behind me, Mom said a silent prayer about them having a safe and uneventful flight. Dee's cell began to ring, and it was Tim. Leon headed into the kitchen for some leftovers while Trish and I sat near Dad and eavesdropped on Dee's conversation. Mom sat down beside Dad and tried to figure out what movie he was watching on the television. The kids had gone upstairs to play games and go on social media.

Dee hung up the phone and decided to tell us what the conversation was about.

"So Tim said he's going to need more time and wants to see if I could stay here with you, Toni," she said, but I could see the pain in her eyes.

"He feels that we need some space before we go to counseling. He also said he'll tell the kids once they get home and that he'll let them call me from time to time," she continued.

"Okay, so how long do you want to stay, or did he want you to stay away from the kids?" It was my turn to ask questions.

"He said at least two to three weeks, and I agreed with that."

I nodded and told her it was fine with me. Houston as a city had a lot for her to see without feeling like she couldn't go anywhere.

"Listen, if you need any help, you can also call me anytime, Dee," Trish chimed in.

"Sis, you're always welcome to stay here. I can rent you a car if you want to go and explore the city," I offered because I knew the last thing she needed was to stay inside thinking about the situation that occurred. When the situation happened with me, I tried to stay busy working so I wouldn't beat myself up about what went wrong and why. With Mom, Dad, and Dee staying here, I felt good inside that I had some normalcy of family around me. Trish and Leon were flying back tomorrow, so I wouldn't be seeing them until Christmas time.

My phone started chiming. It was Natalie, probably calling for the latest gossip with the fam and to check on me.

"Hey, Nat," I spoke into the phone.

"Hey, how are you doing? How was your Thanksgiving?" she asked.

I let her know it was good and walked upstairs into my bedroom for some privacy. I told her about the situation with Dee and her husband and that Dee would be staying with me. I informed her about not going back to work until after the Christmas holiday and that Mom and Dad were staying with me until after Christmas.

"Oh, I know you're glad about that," she shot back.

She couldn't believe that Dee had actually cheated on Tim. She pretty much gasped when I told her. She considered Dee a good friend, so she was shocked, to say the least.

"Girl, that was not on my bingo card for this year," she said, and I could almost picture her big eyes through the phone.

"What is she going to do?"

"Well, she's going to go to marriage counseling, and hopefully they can get back to being in a good place, but it's going to take time."

"Yeah, and I'm wondering if she's ready for that process in itself," Natalie said.

I told her at least Tim was willing to try to work it out and try to forgive her at the same time. The reality was that men often didn't forgive women who cheated on them. Women often forgave easier or were the least likely to leave the relationship. It usually took more than once for a woman to leave. After the second time, I was over trying to make it work with Christian.

I said my goodbyes to Natalie and started reflecting on what forced me to leave—the fact that I saw what I saw in our own house, in our bedroom. I could never get that image out of my mind. Three years later, and I still had that image burned into my memory. I immediately wiped the thoughts away and focused on what I could do for Dee. Even though I'd never cheated on Christian, I knew some of how she was feeling.

I walked down the stairs, and both Mom and Dad were talking amongst each other. Trish and Dee must've gone into the kitchen while I was upstairs on the phone. I walked into the kitchen, and they weren't there. Mom told me they'd left and went out to see the city.

"Oh, okay. I was going to speak to Dee about her getting out of the house since she was going to be here for a while," I said to Mom while I walked to where they were sitting.

"Are you two good?" I asked.

"Yeah, baby, we're just sitting here talking and watching the news on TV," Mom replied.

I sat back in the armchair and tuned into what they were looking at. Several hours later, Trish and Dee walked into the door laughing together. Now that was a good sign.

"I took Dee out to show her some of the city even though I didn't even know where we were going," Trish said through the laughter.

"Dee kept asking me, did I know where I was going? I'm trying to play it cool like I've been here before," Trish continued.

"I didn't know where in the world I was going, but I didn't care. I had to get sis out of this house. I at least had the

GPS on, so we weren't totally lost."

I just sat there and shook my head. I could only imagine the people driving by them, honking their horns, knowing those two didn't know where they were going.

"Trish thought she was fooling me into thinking she knew where we were driving to," Dee chimed in, laughing about it.

"I knew she didn't know where to go, but I sat there and just enjoyed the ride," Dee confessed.

"Well, at least she didn't tell you and make you feel bad," I added.

"Nah, I would never do that. I know my big sis was just trying to make me feel better," Dee said.

"I'm glad she got me out of the house, and we both had a good time in the process. Thank you, Trish, for doing that," Dee added.

"We finally ended up finding this quiet café not too far from here. We went in and were pretty impressed with how the place looked," Trish said.

"I'm glad you guys had a good time, and I know you got to think about something other than what's going on with you and Tim," I said to Dee.

"I really don't want to say goodbye to the kids just yet, but I feel like I don't have a choice," Dee confessed.

As if on cue, Dee's kids came downstairs packed, and I walked to meet them at the stairs. After I gave them hugs and kisses, they went to their mom and gave her hugs and kisses. Tim had come in and said his goodbyes to everyone, including Dee, but did not go over to kiss her. I told Tim to let us know when he and the kids landed safely. He promised he would, and the kids and he left out the door. All of a sudden,

I heard screaming and crying and turned to look in Dee's direction. She was a ball of nerves, to say the least. Mom and Dad rushed over to comfort her, and Trish and I just looked at each other and shook our heads. This was out of our depth of knowledge—Trish had never experienced this, and my situation didn't involve kids. All we could do was comfort her, but we were glad our parents were here to add to the comfort.

As our parents continued to comfort her, I decided to go upstairs and check on my friends, catch up on some good gossip to take my mind off this situation. Natalie, I knew, would have some good gossip. I called her up, and she didn't disappoint. We talked for about twenty good minutes. It was nice to catch up outside of family, and I told her next week we'd get together and go out for some drinks. She asked about the family and how things were going. I told her Dee would be staying here along with Mom and Dad. I summarized what transpired but left out the part of Dee cheating on her husband. She stated she'd say a prayer for their marriage and that she had to go finish up watching her show.

Next on the list was Alexis. I hadn't talked to her since I returned from Bora Bora. We chatted for a while and talked about our families' get-togethers, and I asked her when she'd be out to visit so we could hang out. She said it would be sometime in the early spring since, like Florida, Texas tended to get hot early in the year. I told her I'd definitely clear my schedule for a week when she came to visit. We always had a good time, and she pretty much got along with my other friends.

I checked in on Sandra to see how she was doing and to let her know I was back from vacation. She then told me that my ex-husband had put a for-sale sign on the house. Not surprisingly, I knew he would because he didn't like the house from the start—I did. He told me to my face he'd never sell the house, yet here we were. Sandra also told me he'd told her he was moving to another law firm out of state. I really didn't care at this point, and I told her good for him and that I didn't want to know anything else about him. She knew and asked how the family was and said we had to catch up over drinks or dinner. I told her definitely, it would be before Christmas.

After I hung up, I felt better and returned back downstairs to see what was going on. Dee, Mom, and Dad were still in the same spot. So I decided to take out some food and cook dinner. Trish was in the kitchen fixing some leftovers.

"Girl, this is going to tear her apart mentally. You have to make sure she gets out of the house as much as possible while she's here," Trish reconfirmed.

I nodded in agreement.

"I'll make sure she has somewhere to go each day she's here, at least for an hour a day," I said.

I began to look up museums and places to visit while staying in the area. I came across five museums and a handful of events that were happening this week. Thankfully, it was the holidays, so there was no shortage of events going on in the area. I sat down at the kitchen table and made a list of places to visit, and if Dee wanted me to go along with her, I would.

"Trish, I made a list of places for Dee to visit, and with the holidays around, there are a lot of events going on as well," I said.

Trish nodded and sat down and looked at the places.

"Yes, this looks good, and I'm sure Dee would like it."

I then got up and walked out to the living room and asked everyone if they wanted leftovers for dinner, and everyone nodded. Just then, Leon walked into the kitchen and was talking to Trish about getting packed and ready for the flight in the morning. Trish and he walked upstairs and were talking to the girls about making sure they had everything packed except for what they were wearing to the airport.

As I put food into the oven to warm it up, my phone chimed. It was a text from one of the dating sites I was on. I was intrigued by the profile picture of this person. Now, before I met Christian, I was dating several guys but wasn't in a relationship—it was just for fun. One, though, had my heart from the beginning, and he knew it. However, Christian came on the scene and took over my whole life. Shut everyone and everything down. He immediately was like no dating other people, no male friends, and we were serious from the start. I thought at the beginning this was cute, but now realized it was controlling behavior. The one who had my heart tried to tell me if Christian really wanted a serious relationship, he wouldn't be threatened by other people at all. He told me that wasn't healthy. Him and I had a few sensual sessions, but at the time, both of us were young and weren't looking to get into a relationship. Truth be told, college was our relationship. I chuckled to myself.

As I stared at the profile and picture of the person, I began to wonder if this was the same person I'd met in college. It could very well be him, just an older version of him. My profile stated the college I went to, as his had the same one. I sent him a hello message back and asked a few questions that I knew the guy I was friends with would know. You could never be too careful with online dating because scammers had used people's pictures without their permission. I wanted to know if this was that actual person and not someone looking for some money.

I put the phone down and took out the food from the oven. I then peeked my head into the living room and told everyone the food was ready. By the time I picked my phone up, I had a few messages back from the mystery man. He confirmed the questions I'd asked, and the college was confirmed as well. Oh my goodness, I thought to myself. If this was him, my heart suddenly leaped into my throat. All of those good sessions that neither he nor I could get enough of. I flashed back to moments we'd shared, and shook those thoughts out of my head. I couldn't believe I'd reconnected with him.

I asked him how life was going and where and what he was doing at this point, secretly hoping he wasn't married and was free as well. He said he wasn't married, had gotten a divorce over a year ago, and had two kids. He'd moved to California, outside of San Diego. He said he'd been thinking about me for a while and wondered what happened. He said he never thought in a million years he'd see me on a dating app. I told him I'd been newly divorced and had no kids as of yet. I told him of the hell I went through with Christian. I told him also I was glad to reconnect with him after all these years, and he asked if we could meet up for dinner. I then gave him my direct number so we could exchange text messages and calls.

A long smile spread across my lips when Trish asked who I was texting. I hadn't even realized her and Leon had come back downstairs. It felt like time stopped when I was messaging him.

"I haven't seen a smile like that on you in years, girl. Who were you texting?" she said with intrigue in her voice.

"Well, it seems I've reconnected with a friend from college, and he wants to take me out to dinner," I confessed with a big smile on my face.

Trish was standing beside me trying to see who the person was. I let her see my phone. She was even shocked that I'd reconnected with this person. Trish knew a few of my friends from college because I'd told her a lot back then. Dee also knew this person but didn't really know the details of what happened between us. It was Christian, of course, who made me stop.

"Well, Toni, I know you need to take him up on that dinner. It might be fate that you reconnected with him," Trish said with a genuine smile on her face.

Dee was happy for me, but I could tell she was preoccupied. I then took the opportunity to give Dee the list and told her if she needed me to go with her to any of these, just let me know. She gave me a big hug and told me thanks.

I looked at Dee and told her at this point to put this in God's hands—we could only control what we could. She looked at me with tears in her eyes and said she really appreciated me and that Mom and Dad were here to help her get through this.

I then grabbed a plate and sat down at the table with Trish and Leon. The kids came down and grabbed some food and sat down with us. I looked at my phone and got a direct text from him with a nice-looking picture—the same as his profile picture, thankfully. His name was Eric. He stood at six-four, and his body was a work of art. He had a brown caramel complexion, muscles everywhere, and a regular low-cut haircut. His eyes were slanted, and people used to ask him in college if he was mixed with Asian. He'd often worked out and played soccer in college.

I sent him a picture of me. He texted back that I looked

the same and then asked when he could fly out to meet me for dinner. I said I was free pretty much the week after Christmas if he wanted to make it a New Year's Eve get-together. He agreed and said he looked forward to seeing me. His picture brought back all sorts of memories, and another smile came over my face.

"Toni, you are literally blushing at this point. I hope you took him up on his offer," Trish inquired.

"I did," I replied back with an even bigger smile on my face. It felt so good to be expectant about romance once again.

"Good," she shot back.

I was so excited now. I wanted Christmas to hurry up and come so I could see him. He was now a sports agent with his own business. Thinking to myself, this was definitely someone I'd want to reconnect with after being on such a long hiatus. The things we'd done while in college. We could've been the main characters of a romance movie. We'd been open to anything but also young. I wouldn't go there now because I was older and needed some type of discretion since my career had me out in the public... But the memories lingered.

Everyone was now sitting around the table enjoying some of the leftover Thanksgiving food. Mom and Dad said their goodnights and proceeded to retire into one of the bedrooms. Me, Leon, and Trish sat around enjoying some small talk while Dee got up and started doing the dishes. Leon and Trish said their goodnights and proceeded to go upstairs. Dee finished up the dishes, and we sat around for a couple more hours talking. She was feeling uncertain about continuing her marriage to Tim. Her mindset right now was all over the place. She felt so guilty for stepping outside of the marriage. I tried to reassure her that if she found out counseling wasn't working out, we as the family would have her back, like they'd had my back.

Both of us decided to call it a night, and she headed upstairs while I cut out the lights and television. Then I walked upstairs and collapsed on the bed, thinking about seeing Eric again. The next morning, Trish and Leon came into the bedroom to wake me up so I could see them and the kids off. I jumped into the shower, got dressed while they were getting last-minute items packed. The kids had already gone downstairs and were watching television. After throwing on some clothes, I walked downstairs and kissed the kids goodbye and hugged both Trish and Leon. They all walked out of the door, and I saw them get into the vehicle.

Mom and Dad shortly came down the stairs, and I told them Trish and they had already left. They both went into the kitchen to start on the coffee brewing. I told Mom and Dad both that Trish would text me once they landed at the airport.

"Toni, do you want us to brew you some coffee?" Dad asked, this time doing the brew assignment instead of Mom.

"Yes, I would."

I knew I'd be up anyway, catching up on some emails and sorting through the potential client list. I knew the new year would be approaching quickly, so I wanted to line up potential buyers and sellers for the first three months of the year. Mom, Dad, and I sat around engaged in light conversation when Dee came into the kitchen.

"How are you doing, honey?" Dad asked.

"I'm taking it one day at a time. I think I'm going to fix breakfast for you guys, and then I'm going out to one of the art shows in town," Dee said, looking noticeably less stressed than the day before.

Mom chimed in, "Oh, that sounds wonderful. Would you like some company?"

"No, I want to be alone for a while, just to feel what it is to be without someone by your side."

We all nodded, and Dee started going into the refrigerator and preparing to make breakfast. I hadn't had Dee's cooking in a long time, so I was delighted and couldn't wait to try it. She'd made us omelets, and I must say, I was impressed.

"This looks so good, Dee," Mom said, and the rest of us nodded in agreement.

We sat around the table engaging in small talk while we ate.

"Okay, I'm heading upstairs to change into some casual clothes, and I'll see you guys later," Dee said as she was getting up from the table.

"Besides, I have a long day of sightseeing ahead of me and don't want to waste any more time."

After putting her dish in the sink, she walked out of the kitchen and up the stairs. Alright then, I thought to myself. I sat around for a little longer talking to Mom and Dad. Then I told them I had to do a bit of work for a while and I'd see them later. They both nodded and continued their conversation. I always looked up to my parents. I wanted a marriage like theirs—communication was so important. I knew for a fact there were times when they were upset with each other, but they would always talk it out when they were calmer.

Once I sat down in the chair in my office, I looked through some emails on my laptop. Right on cue, my assistant, Layla, called me and asked how I was doing. I told her I was doing good and glad to have my parents here with me after not seeing them for so long. We continued to talk for about thirty minutes, and I told her I'd be ready to get back into the work groove the first week of January. Might as well start the year off building as many clients as possible. She confirmed a few potential clients for that first week and into the middle of January. Awesome, I thought to myself.

The divorce didn't have any hiccups like I was expecting, which was why I'd taken the break I needed. I only wanted to maintain my business, and since he didn't personally put any funding toward the business, he didn't have assets in it. I didn't want any of his assets or even the ones we'd bought when we'd married. I let him keep all of that, and I think that was why he didn't protest as much—since he made off pretty well in the divorce. My parents had my back and told me that even though they were retired, they'd make sure I didn't need any financial assistance from him. They wanted the situation to end as quickly as possible. However, I confirmed to them business was booming, and if I needed any help, it would be very limited. I also deep down thought that was why he secretly resented my business. He was hoping it would fail so I'd come back or find an excuse to come back into his life.

I continued scrolling through the emails and started gathering the listings that would be coming up for the first month of the new year. The housing market so far had done exactly what the analysis said it would. The interest rates fell again, and that meant a surplus of housing and a surplus of buyers. I was excited for both because this might just be my biggest year yet. I was the sole owner of my business, but I still had a managing partner I'd brought on about five years ago. Jim proved he had just as much ambition as I did and continued to bring in clients looking for investment properties. I also had two realtors who worked under Jim and me. Tia and Gina were both excellent at selling and at the same time making sure they took care of their existing buyers. The four of us were unstoppable, and each year the business kept growing. If this year turned out like I thought it would, I might have to add on two more agents to the roster.

As much as I liked the money coming in and the business growing, I still wanted my agents to have a healthy work-life balance in this business. It was easy to become burnt out, like I almost did when I first started. That was partly because I didn't want to spend any more time at home than I had to be around Christian. I quickly realized that wasn't healthy, though. Jim literally came into my life at the right time, and I'd never regretted it. Thinking back on how we met—I was at the store looking for certain items and ended up being frustrated because I couldn't find them. Seeing the frustration on my face, Jim asked what it was I was looking for. He instantly found it, and we introduced ourselves after I thanked him for not making me feel like I'd lost my mind. I found out he was also a broker, and I told him I'd just started my own real estate agency. He then said he was actually in between agencies since he and the previous owner had a disagreement. I told him to come in on Monday, and we'd discuss if he'd be a good fit for my company. The rest, as they say, was history. He had his own list of clients and investors, and we really got along great. It was the perfect fit. He didn't need management at all. We'd been tight ever since. He knew about the divorce and that whole process, and I often came to him for advice since he'd been through that situation years ago. Him and my parents' advice in that area were spot on. He often told me just leave with the business that way I wouldn't need him to do anything or hold out just because he wanted to spite me.

After making the listings of houses and checking through most of the emails, I closed the laptop and went back into the living room where my parents were. Mom asked if everything was okay, and I told her everything was coming together great for the coming year. I was looking forward to a great year. Dad told me how proud he was of me and wanted nothing but the best for his baby girl.

"Hey, Toni, we're going to get out of your hair for a bit and go out sightseeing ourselves," Dad said with Mom nodding in the background.

"We're going to have an Uber come pick us up and take us to catch a football game," he continued.

"Okay, that sounds good. Please be careful out there," I said.

Dad nodded and said they would. I worried about them since they were in an unfamiliar area. After they shut the front door, I looked out the window to make sure they were okay. Just then, my cell phone rang, and it was Trish. She told me they'd landed safely and were driving to their house. I told them Dee and our parents went out to sightsee, and I was actually in the house by myself. She laughed and said that was a good thing. She said Leon and the kids were super tired, and she was the one driving them to the house like she wasn't tired herself. I told her I was sure she lost that vote as soon as she asked who was driving. We both laughed, and I told them I loved them and hung up the phone.

Then, out of the blue, Paul texted and asked how I was doing, checking in on me and how the holiday celebrations were going. I texted back that everything was going good and that the new year looked very promising business-wise. I also asked how he was doing and how his family was doing. He, of course, asked when I'd get around to making time to see him since he'd be in New York around April and asked if I could meet up then. I was on the fence about meeting up with him. Besides, we'd had a good time in Bora Bora, but I'd emphasized that I was only looking to date. I wasn't at all looking for a relationship, and even if I was, with him being across the water, how was that going to work? What would that even look like? Would we split time between summer in the United States and the fall in the U.K.? I mean, that was a lot to consider. I had to think long and hard about how far I wanted our potential friendship to go.

I told Paul that I would visit, but I had to be honest and tell him I didn't think I could take this any further than the dating stage. He texted back that he understood and to just come and visit first before I decided. I agreed and told him that in the first week of May, I'd clear my schedule and make sure to be there in New York. Thinking to myself, was this really something I wanted to pursue? It was uncertain, risky, and scary all at the same time.

A few hours later, I started preparing dinner as it was getting late. I dialed up Mom and asked what time the game would be ending. She stated another hour or so and not to worry about fixing dinner for them as they'd grabbed something to eat while they were at the stadium. Almost at the same time, Dee had called to tell me she was on her way home, and I asked her if she'd like dinner since I was cooking something to eat. After hanging up the phone with Mom, I clicked back to Dee, and she told me to make her a plate. She asked where our parents had gone to, and I told her they went to one of the college football games. She said she was almost home, and so I hung up the phone.

I heard the car pulling into the driveway, so I went to the front door to unlock it.

"So how do you like the city so far?" I asked.

Dee walked into the living room and looked much better than she had in the past few days.

"Oh, I had such a good time going around to the art museums. I even stopped by this shop that had some good ideas for crafting."

"Well, that sounds promising," I said as I went back into the kitchen to finish up our food.

Dee came into the kitchen and said everything smelled good. She hadn't realized she was that hungry. Then she realized she hadn't eaten anything since earlier that morning.

"I guess I was so caught up in the sights and taking time out for me that I'm hungrier than I thought."

I made some fish tacos with a side of rice and refried beans. I could eat refried beans all day if I wanted to—I loved the way they tasted. I also had some grilled asparagus as the vegetable. Dee told me she'd talked to Tim, and they'd reached a compromise on when she would return home. Instead of the five days, Tim and her decided three days was enough to stay out here with me. Not to mention that the kids were asking almost every day when their mom was coming home. At their ages, they knew their mother being gone wasn't right. I told Dee it was good that they were able to talk it out. There was still hope for their marriage.

Dee and I sat down and talked some more while we were eating. Mom and Dad had rung the doorbell, and this time Dee got up to go to the door. Dee, Mom, and Dad were talking about the football game as they walked toward the kitchen. Both Mom and Dad were describing how the game went with excitement in their voices. It was so comforting to see them so happy together, as if they didn't have a care in the world. I told them both I was glad they'd had a great time at the game. Dee also told them the good news that she'd be leaving in two more days instead of four more days.

"Oh, baby, that's a good sign right there," Dad said.

Mom agreed and said a silent prayer that they'd be able to heal and move on from this situation. Dee was so excited that Tim had a change of heart, and hopefully with time, he'd be able to forgive her. Mom and Dad decided since they'd had so much excitement after the game, they were going upstairs to retire for the evening. Dee and I sat around and talked, and I asked her what plans she had for tomorrow.

"I was thinking of finding that nice café that Trish and I ran into before."

I nodded and said I'd like to go with her this time if she wanted some company.

"Yes, I would like some company. I don't feel like eating by myself," Dee stated.

"Okay, just let me know what time, and I can drive you there without having to worry about getting lost," I said as I laughed out loud.

Dee laughed with me, thinking back to Trish trying to find the place by U-turning at least three times. We both said our goodnights and went upstairs to go to bed. I sank into the bed for a well-deserved sleep. Even though I knew Dee had everything under control, I still worried about her and the future of her marriage. I really didn't think Tim wanted a divorce, he was feeling hurt; he never thought his wife would find comfort in the arms of another man. Dee was human, though, after all, and we make mistakes. Trust me, I'd been tempted more than one time and by more than one person. They knew deep down that I wasn't happy in the marriage and hadn't been for a long time. I just refused to give up because it felt like I was quitting. Thankfully, Dad told me a long time ago that sometimes quitting wasn't failing—it was another form of trying again or starting over. Mentally, though, I had to get that into my thoughts. I had to get to a place where I wouldn't feel bad by throwing in the towel, as they say.

Falling asleep, I had a crazy dream that Dee had turned into a killer and stabbed Tim and her kids. Note to self—never eat chips late at night again.

6

A Bitter Aftertaste

The following morning, I awoke to the sounds chatter coming from downstairs. I still wasn't used to noise early in the morning, even if it was family. I jumped into the shower and afterward threw on a pink long-sleeved shirt and some black jeans. I decided to put on a pair of black tennis shoes to go along with the jeans. Once I arrived in the kitchen, I saw Dee, Dad, and Mom talking about the news. Mom had coffee duty this morning, but I declined. Dee said she was ready to go to the café and told our parents we'd be back probably in a couple of hours. I told them to reach out by cell if they needed anything while we were out. Being independent as they were, our parents said they were good and would stay at the house enjoying the television. We each hugged them both and walked toward the door.

Once in the car, Dee started the conversation.

"Toni, I know Mom and Dad are just looking out for me, but I don't need to be babied."

"Well," I said, "you're saying that because they've been in your life constantly. I haven't been around, and trust me, you miss them fussing over you. They're only looking out for you because they really love you and don't want to see you go through what I went through. Not saying it will happen just like that." I almost lost my train of thought, hoping that last response made sense.

"You're right, Toni," she agreed, then continued, "When you weren't present during those years, it really left a void in the family. You have no idea how depressed Mom and Dad had become after you weren't contacting them on a consistent basis. Kevin, Trish, and I had to rally around them to let them know not to give up and that we were still in their lives no matter what."

Dee sat back in the seat as I started the car, and we proceeded to drive toward where the café was.

"Then when Kevin told them he had a job opportunity in California, they were less than thrilled, but they understood," she continued. "They didn't know when or if ever they would see you again, and then Kevin was moving basically across the country. Kevin had to reassure them that he would call and visit as much as he could."

After hearing her say that, I retreated back into my thoughts. I knew none of this, and it made me feel powerless to do anything to change it. We got out of the car and went into the café. I ordered a Colombian brew, and Dee ordered a macchiato. We then ordered breakfast sandwiches and muffins. Sitting down, Dee told me she and Tim had talked for a long time yesterday, and he said he missed her and wanted her to come home sooner. She also said he'd made several appointments with the marriage counselor and texted her the dates and times of when they'd be going there. I told her I was happy he was learning to work around the mistake and that he would eventually forgive her. Both the food and coffee were delicious.

Dee then said she'd like to walk around the park she'd noticed while her and Trish were out. We talked for several minutes more when my phone started ringing. It was Natalie. I spoke into the phone, and Natalie said, "Guess what," in an excited voice. I replied back because I knew by the tone of her voice this was some juicy tea. She started telling me about the charge nurse who'd basically been harassing her since they shared the same shift together. Well, something happened on the charge nurse's watch, and she ended up being on disciplinary action behind what had occurred. Natalie was almost grinning from ear to ear as she continued with the story. Apparently, the charge nurse was covering for one of her friends on shift by clocking her in and out whenever her friend showed up late. She made sure the friend would have all the overtime needed, and when Natalie would ask for extra hours, the charge nurse would tell her there weren't any. The nurse had lied and then went behind Natalie's back to her boss and told them that Natalie was turning down shift work and didn't want to work any extra hours.

Natalie ended up going into her boss's office to defend herself, but they were already aware of the charge nurse helping out the friend because the other staff members were complaining as well, and they'd started documenting when it happened. My mouth by this time was hanging open because I couldn't believe Miss Holier-than-Thou herself had gotten busted.

Natalie and this lady had a long history together, and even though she treated Natalie like shit, Natalie ignored her most of the time and did the work better than expected so no one could say anything about her work ethic. I'd met the charge nurse a couple of times when I would come up to Natalie's job as she was finishing out her shift. She immediately rubbed me the wrong way. Natalie just couldn't believe she no longer would be on the same shift anymore. I told Natalie I was happy that issue was no more. My best friend hadn't really been herself lately because that woman was micromanaging everything Natalie did. I knew she'd wanted to tell me a few times what was going on, but she realized I had my own issues with what I'd gone through. I told Natalie that if she needed a listening ear, despite what I had going on, I would always be there. She told me she knew that, but she really couldn't say much while they were investigating the situation with the nurse in question.

After saying I'd call her back, she insisted we needed to meet to have a mini celebration. She told me it felt like a weight had been lifted from her chest, and she felt like she could be free to be herself again. I told her Dee was going back by Sunday, and we could get together then for drinks. Dee had a bunch of questions when I put down the phone.

"What in the world was that about?" she asked.

"Apparently her charge nurse got busted for showing favoritism with one of Natalie's coworkers at the job, chile."

"Oh wow, that's good, I'm sure, on Natalie's part."

"Yes, because this woman didn't like Natalie and made it known she was trying to get rid of her. She even told her boss that Natalie was turning down work and didn't want to help with overtime."

"Oh, I know she's lying now," Dee emphasized with disbelief on her face.

"We all know she's lying. Girl, Natalie doesn't turn down any extra work. That's not even in her, unless she has an emergency she can't get out of or she's really tired and needs to sleep. Meanwhile, she was hooking her best friend up with almost unlimited hours," I told all of this to Dee.

"Natalie hadn't told me when it started because she couldn't talk about it until after everything was out in the open and the nurse was written up," I said, shaking my head.

Dee and I got up from the table and went toward the car. I set the GPS for going to the park I knew Trish and her were talking about. Dee said she was glad to be here with me—even though she missed her kids and husband, this was a welcome break. I had a feeling she needed a break more than she'd let on. We arrived at the park and started on our hike. I missed this so much. I was glad to have her here to talk to while we hiked. I'd visited this part more than a few times, especially when my stress was at an all-time high. However, it was different when you had someone to just talk to without judgment. Dee knew I was far from perfect, even though the perception of me was different. From the outside, people thought I had everything together. They didn't realize the last four years of my life were pure hell. I wouldn't wish that on my worst enemy. Dee knew this and didn't judge me on what happened. Despite me not heeding the warnings, the whole family was supportive in my decision. There were red flags throughout the marriage, but I thought I had to suffer for the longevity of the marriage. As long as I had him, I didn't care who he chose to sleep with. I was suffering inside, though.

"Whew, this walking is definitely what I needed," Dee said, interrupting my internal thoughts.

"Yes, I needed this intense walk to clear my mind as well," I nodded, and we continued on the trail for at least an hour.

"Whew," we both let out a sigh at almost the same time after we'd walked back to the car.

"Thank you, sis. That was a good walk," Dee said as she was patting her face with a towel.

"You're welcome. Maybe if you come back for Christmas, we can do this walk again."

"Yeah, I'd like that," Dee confirmed.

Getting into the car after our water break, we decided to go to the nearest eatery to have a light snack. That walk had both of us feeling hungry but not starving. We arrived at the local juice bar spot that had both smoothies and salads. I decided to get a salad, and Dee ordered a nice berry smoothie. We sat down and talked for a little bit while we ate our food— or in her case, drank the food. I'd gotten a nice chicken salad on a bed of lettuce while Dee had a smoothie with strawberries, blueberries, and raspberries with a hint of banana.

Suddenly, Dee's phone rang, and picking it up, I noticed she had a surprised look on her face. It was her oldest, Brad, on the phone. I was sort of eavesdropping without being too obvious. Dee kept saying yes and nodding, and I wanted to know so bad what was said. I was dying a slow death trying to hear. After hanging up the phone, Dee saw my anticipation in my eyes and started spilling what the conversation was about. Brad didn't have much to say but to tell his mom whatever she needed to do to fix the situation. He'd even started cooking for his siblings because they didn't like Dad's cooking. Dee was kind of surprised as she was telling me this. Brad never missed his mom like he did now. I told Dee the kids would always miss her, and sometimes they didn't know it until she wasn't in their life every day. I also agreed with the kids that they always needed their mom, and whatever was going to happen to this marriage, they'd still need their mom after it.

Driving back to the house, Dee and I sat in silence with our thoughts. Opening the door, Mom greeted us first since she was in the living room looking at television.

"How was your outing?"

"It was eventful," Dee said and proceeded to walk over to the sofa and sit down beside our mom.

"Mom, Brad called me and said I had to come back ASAP. He can't take anymore of Tim's cooking," Dee smirked because she began to realize for once she was needed.

Mom started laughing as soon as she said it.

"My son-in-law's cooking must be pretty bad for Brad to complain about it."

Dee nodded.

"Yeah, because I swear my son will eat anything that isn't nailed down in the house."

"Isn't that the truth? He practically tore through the turkey at Thanksgiving by himself," Mom laughed, recalling how hungry Brad was.

By this time, Dad walked into the living room, joining in the conversation.

"That boy is growing, and his appetite is doing most of the work. Which means, Dee, you may have to have a small fortune put aside for his shoe wear."

Dee chimed in, "I know, Dad."

I decided to go into the kitchen and prepare lunch since I was sure everyone was hungry. I baked some chicken with a side of string beans and potato salad. Dee ate quickly and then went upstairs to start packing. She missed her kids and Tim more than she let on. I secretly worried about her. She put on a brave face, but I knew she was going through it mentally and emotionally. Meanwhile, I was just waiting for the Christmas holiday to approach and also to see Eric. I never thought we would reconnect again. He was coming through right after the Christmas holiday, and he might stay to celebrate New Year's Eve with me. I was hoping he would, anyway. I knew that would be an incredible night to remember. I couldn't wait either.

Mom and Dad ate and went back into the living room looking at whatever they were finishing up on the television. Dee appeared in the kitchen, and we sat down and talked.

"I'm not going to lie, Toni. I miss my kids. I miss Tim also, but I know there is a lot we need to discuss and get out in the open. You know Trish texts me every day and asks how I'm feeling. She knows I'm going through it, so she also sends words of encouragement. That helps out more than she knows, Toni."

I just sat there and let Dee vent and let her sort her feelings out. I knew this was what she needed, and I wanted her to know this was a judgment-free zone. I had no place to judge and definitely didn't want her to feel uncomfortable talking to me after we hadn't spoken in the last several years of my marriage. I listened to her feelings about the person she'd slept with. She downplayed it like it didn't mean anything, but I knew better. The truth was, once you crossed that line, you couldn't undo it. Everyone knew that. You always left a piece of yourself with that person, whether it was acknowledged or not—it still happened. She trusted me with knowing she'd crossed a line with someone who was basically a stranger, which I guess was better than someone she knew. Tim, though, didn't see it that way. The act itself betrayed the trust he had in her to be faithful—which was what I'd felt but without the acknowledgment from Christian that what he did was wrong. Total denial. Dee, on the other hand, knew what she did was wrong and took accountability for the situation.

"Thanks for listening and letting me vent about what I'm going through," Dee continued. "I know Tim and I will get back on the right track. It's just the unknown of how and when that has me worried. That one-night stand didn't mean anything. I had no feelings involved with that person."

I interjected, "Tim isn't thinking about that part. He's thinking about the physical act itself and what it means."

"I know, and in his mind, that's what's eating at him," Dee said.

I continued to listen until Dee told me she was going to lay down for a while. I stayed in the kitchen cleaning up and putting away the leftovers from earlier. I glanced down at my phone, and Eric had texted me the details of his flight information and the hotel he'd be at. I then knew he was more excited than I was about looking forward to getting together again. I wanted to know all about his life after we both graduated from college. I wasn't sure he'd want to know about what happened in my life after college. That would be what some people would consider "baggage." I'd tell him in due time. It would definitely depend on how well we reconnected this time around.

I went into the living room, and Dad and Mom both said they were going to turn in for the night since it was late. For them, any time after seven PM was late. I sat down to see what I could find to look at on the television. Realizing it was getting late for me, I decided to pull out the current book I was reading and read a few pages. I wasn't yet sleepy, and there was no need to force sleep to come. After reading a few pages, I nodded off on the sofa without realizing it. I woke up to what I thought I heard was the back door being shut, but I got up and went into the kitchen and noticed the back door was still locked. Must've been a dream, I thought to myself. I glanced at the wall clock, and it was three o'clock in the morning. I stumbled a bit up the stairs and proceeded to go toward my bedroom. I checked on everyone by peeping in the other bedrooms, and everyone was sound asleep. I took a quick shower and then slid into the bed, feeling the soft covers embrace my tired body.

A New Lure

The next day, waking up later than usual, I heard the familiar voices downstairs. I took a shower and put on clothes to go to the dance studio. I knew today was the last day Dee would be here. Her flight was tonight, and I deep down would miss her presence in the house. As I walked down the stairs, I smelled the familiar scent of pancakes and bacon being cooked. Mom must've gotten a taste for wanting some good breakfast this morning instead of just toast and coffee. I walked into the kitchen where everyone else was and made myself a plate.

"You must've wanted some good food, Mom. This looks delicious," I said.

"Yes, it does," Dee agreed.

"I thought we would have a good breakfast since this is Dee's last day with us," Mom chimed in.

I sat down at the table after grabbing my plate and

dug into the food. Dee and Mom were talking about what time her flight left, and Dad was glancing at his cell phone, probably reading the news. I told both of our parents I was going to go to dance class and would be back shortly after I ran some errands. I asked them if they were going to go out anywhere, and they both said they were going to catch another football game. They told Dee and me they'd be back in time to take her to the airport, but Dee said she would get an Uber to take her. I nodded and kissed Mom and Dad and left out the door for the dance class. I was meeting Natalie there. Natalie came to the class every other week since her schedule at the hospital changed sometimes daily.

Once at the dance class, Natalie spoke, and I walked over to where she was.

"Hey, girl, I am so glad you're here," I said. "I have so much to tell you, and it was too much to talk about over the phone or text," I continued.

As we put our bags and towels in the lockers, we gathered to start the dance routines. I'd joined this class as soon as I moved closer to where Natalie worked. Usually, she would go either in between shifts if she was feeling extra stressed or in the mornings along with me on her way into work. We started several dance routines, and both of us were starting to feel better. As class was wrapping up, Natalie and I went toward the back near the lockers and started talking.

"Dee got a call from her oldest son and said she needed to come home ASAP because Tim cannot cook, and he missed her cooking."

Natalie burst out laughing as she listened to more of the conversation.

"Girl, Brad sounds desperate. He swore he was losing too much weight and his clothes were getting too big."

"Noooo," Natalie responded. "He sounded serious. Poor thing," she continued. "He probably doesn't want to hurt his dad's feelings but doesn't want to eat what he cooks either," she continued while laughing as I was speaking.

"He practically begged his mom to get an earlier flight so they could have a good Sunday dinner," I said through tears from laughing.

Natalie literally hollered laughing this time. As Natalie was shaking her head, I started laughing too.

"Your family is a trip," she said.

I agreed because as much as we were close, the drama tended to run high. We said our goodbyes as class was ending, and I walked to my car. She told me she'd text me later so we could get together for some drinks later on in the week. That class was such a good workout and something I needed to get me focused for the upcoming year.

As I drove home, I received a call from my friend Jaden.

"Hello there, friend," I said on the Bluetooth.

She shared news about a brand new area opening up a lot of houses not too far from my office. I liked how she was always in the know when it came to housing projects. I tried to keep up with the up-and-coming housing market, but let's face it, there was a plethora of changes to keep up with. Jaden had a few clients who were investment professionals, so of course that was what kept her knowing what projects and release dates. She also told me about a few projects on the commercial real estate side and asked if I'd thought about getting into that arena. I told her I would leave that part to her. I had enough on my plate with clients' needs, desires, and wants. No way could I add commercial real estate since that was a whole different set of clients and adding in their wants, needs, and desires. Jaden liked challenges, though. I told her good luck and to let me know how that turned out.

I then stopped by the dry cleaners, the grocery store, and the post office to check on my P.O. box. As I pulled into the driveway, I called Dad to come and help with the groceries. I'd only bought a few items just to make sure if Mom wanted to bake something, she wouldn't have to worry about running out and trying to navigate to the store. They were old school, so they didn't trust strangers, as they said, to pick up groceries for them using Instacart. They didn't even like doing the pickup service, which I loved, because they didn't trust that the store associates would pick out the right food. It's always a battle with them sometimes, I said to myself. On one hand, though, I got it. On the other, I was like, change is good.

Walking into the house, I saw Mom and Dee in the living room talking over the movie they were looking at. Dee asked if I needed help with the bags. I told her I didn't—it wasn't that many. Dad brought the rest of the bags in, and I started putting the items away. Dee came into the kitchen and said she was packed and just waiting for the Uber driver to get her. We gathered around and each gave her a hug. Mom and I told her to call or text when she landed. Dee and Tim lived about five hours from our parents, which wasn't as close as Trish and Leon. They lived the closest to our parents, so they saw them more than the rest of us did. I'd thought a few times about moving back to the East Coast, but I liked it in Texas. I had a support system here, not to mention a built-up clientele that kept the flow of income steady. In this business, your reputation and referrals were really all you had.

Dee looked down, checking her phone, and the Uber driver had arrived. We reassured Dee that things would be okay between her and Tim. Though she would hate to admit it, Dee often handled conflict by running away. So during the whole situation, I'd noticed her anxiety had kicked into overtime. As Dad hugged her again at the door, she had a few tears in her eyes and walked outside toward where the Uber driver was. Closing the door, Mom, Dad, and I just stared at each other for a minute. I went into the kitchen and started on the shrimp tacos. Mom walked into the kitchen and started talking to remove the awkward feeling in the air.

"She's going to be alright, Toni. I know in my heart she will be," Mom said.

"I know, but I just can't help feeling bad for her having to go through this," I replied.

"I know, but life is like that. Life is full of lessons that we either have to go through or we have to learn from."

As I continued cooking, by this time Dad had come in and sat at the table. I made plates of food for each of us. Out of the blue, as I sat down, Paul texted me and asked how I was doing and how the family was doing. I replied back and asked him the same. I often wondered if he thought about me or was he just trying to keep the conversation going until we saw each other again. I honestly didn't think about him as someone with long-term potential, and a lot of that had to do with the distance between us. I couldn't say for sure if I wanted to pursue something deeper with him until we met again and saw where we would go from there. I had a better chance of reestablishing a relationship with Eric than with Paul. If, and that was a big *if,* I decided to move to where Paul was, I would be starting my business over again. I didn't know if I was willing to do that. I would have to rebuild brand-new clientele in a whole other country. I pondered since he did some business in this country, would he be willing to relocate here? If so, would he even want to move to Texas, or since he was so familiar with New York, would he prefer we move there instead? There was a lot of uncertainty and definitely lots to sort through before deciding on possibly getting serious.

I turned my attention back to Mom and Dad and asked them how the game was. We'd all been so wrapped up in Dee leaving, no one mentioned the football game. They both chimed in and relayed the highlights of the game. I just listened as I watched their eyes lit up recounting who made which plays in the game. This was what I missed most from my parents—just sitting and vibing with them. I was glad I was back in their lives after what seemed like an eternity of not being around.

Just then Mom's cell phone rang. While on speaker, Dee let us know she'd landed and had an Uber driver was taking her to the house. We told her to keep in touch and to keep us updated. We then jumped right back into the conversation at hand. That convo lasted several more hours when for the final time I said I was going to go to bed and this time I meant it. Dad said okay and that he'd get the dishes. Mom walked into the living room and looked for a movie to find. Between worrying about Dee's situation and dance class, I was beaten mentally and physically. I took a quick shower and slid into the comforting sheets. My dreams were already starting to be a bit strange. Change up my diet again, I said as my thoughts drifted away to a full sleep.

I slowly opened my eyes as the bright sun was peeking through the curtains. I slowly sat up in bed and just shook my head over last night's dream. It was so real, or at least felt that way. I was sitting in a restaurant, almost by myself, and in walked Eric. He sat down and basically laid out his feelings for me. I told him I felt the same way. Then all of a sudden, the background changed, and we were back at what seemed like a hotel room. He walked over to some sort of closet, and all sorts of toys were hanging up. He pulled this ribbon from the closet, and I was sitting in a chair. He then took the ribbon and tied me to the chair and took another ribbon and blindfolded me. Before he blindfolded me, I looked down at myself, and I was wearing a black lace lingerie top and lace panties. I felt his hands running up and down my body. I felt my wetness through my underwear, and his touch brought shivers that ran up and down my body. He then kissed me and began to undress me. As he slid the panties off, he stuck his tongue out and gently sucked on my clit. A wave of feelings came over me as I missed having this intense feeling. I was suddenly awakened by the bright sun and the sound of my parents talking downstairs.

Note to self—put some more furniture in the house to minimize the echoes. I hopped out of the bed and jumped into the shower. It was Monday, and nothing was really on the agenda except checking in to see what Mom and Dad's plans were. After throwing on a nice short-sleeve yellow top and some shorts, I walked downstairs into the kitchen to see what was going on. Mom yelled as soon as I peeked into the kitchen.

"Trish is on the phone and has your dad and me in stitches laughing."

I nodded and proceeded to get some leftover breakfast from the refrigerator. I noticed there was coffee made and thought to myself I'd never used the coffee machine this much. Only my parents, I smiled to myself. I just looked at them both as I warmed up the breakfast casserole Mom had made. I missed having breakfast like this already prepared when usually I had to cook it myself. Thinking back to that dream, it was hot and heavy indeed. Dang, wished that sunlight didn't wake me up. It made me even more excited that Eric was coming to see me. The week couldn't go fast enough. Christmas was three days away, and I knew Trish and Leon were coming back. I was unsure about Kevin, Dee, and Tim. Knowing Dee, she would come back with the kids even if Tim wasn't with her.

I decided to text Kevin and ask him if he was coming back this way for Christmas. I then reached out to Dee to see if they had plans to come back out this way. Kevin texted me back, saying he'd be there Christmas Eve. While on the phone, I overheard Mom asking Trish if they were flying back this way for Christmas. I heard her say yes, they'd all be there, and said this time they would book a hotel suite. I knew they were flying back in for me. The years of not seeing them had them trying to make up for lost time.

"Toni, Mom and I are going for a walk around the neighborhood. It seems so nice outside, and then we may walk to that café you guys have been talking about," Dad looked at me, smiling, and Mom nodded in agreement.

"Okay, you guys just text me before you're on your way back home, so if I go anywhere, I can come home and make sure the door is unlocked," I nodded.

They got up and went to change into comfortable clothes and shoes as it was already muggy out. By this time, I'd put up the food and washed the dishes in the sink. I told them I'd see them later and saw them walk out the front door.

They both had on hats and shorts and short sleeves.

"Okay, you two, be careful out there," I said, closing the door behind me.

I decided to find something on the television to look at. Dee texted me and said it would be her and the kids for Christmas. I thought to myself, fair enough. Tim was probably going to his parents' home for Christmas. I was sure he had a lot to update them on if he hadn't already. I asked Dee how the kids were holding up. "Better than I am," she texted back. I instantly found a good movie on the television. I became immersed in the storyline, and before I knew it, an hour or so had passed by. Mom was calling.

"Hello."

Mom was letting me know they'd made it to the café and were impressed by the menu. She told me they'd be back home in another hour or two. After hanging up, my girl Natalie called.

"Sure, you can come over. My parents walked to the café up the street, so I actually have the house to myself."

Natalie said she'd be over in ten minutes. Shaking my head, I finally got back into the movie. I was tempted to rewind it to see what I'd missed but decided against that. Ringgggggg. I got up and walked toward the door to open it for Natalie. We hugged and then walked over to sit and chat on the sofa.

"I am so glad that bitch is gone. I literally cried tears this morning coming off my shift," Natalie said as she looked at me with joy in her eyes.

I hadn't seen her this happy in a long time.

"She would purposely harass me and the other nurses just because she was miserable at home. I never brought my home life into the job, and because I had a good attitude, she made it her mission to make me miserable."

Natalie seemed to have held those thoughts and feelings in for a long time. I told her she could've come to me anytime, or Jaden, and expressed how she was feeling.

"I know I should've talked to you about this, but I didn't want to add to what you were already going through with the divorce. I didn't want to be a burden."

"You aren't a burden, and I wanted you to tell me what was on your mind. I knew you weren't happy, and I didn't understand why you never said anything."

"You're right. I know going forward I need to vent and not hold it in. It's only hurting me when I do that."

We embraced each other as we sat on the sofa for a while.

"Toni, I was feeling so defeated that I would avoid her at all costs. I didn't want to be at work, and I had even started looking for other job positions."

"Oh, I am so sorry you had to go through that, but it did work out for the best."

I then got up and made some margaritas for the both of us. Nat definitely needed it more than I did. I came back out into the living room and placed both glasses on the table.

"Oh my God, you must've read my mind."

Mom texted me and said they were almost to the house. I walked over to the door and unlocked it.

"So tell me what's been happening with this new man you met on the dating site."

"Oh, he is such a sweetheart. We went out last night, and he looked like his profile picture, thank God."

"Well, yeah, that's a good thing," I said. "You know how many people put up either old pictures or totally different pictures than what they actually look like. That should be against the law."

"Speaking of which, Nat, the time is moving so slow. I am so ready to see Eric again. I'm not going to lie—it's been too long since a man has held me in his arms in bed. I mean, I have my toys, but it's not the same connection that I need."

"Toni, I agree, and I definitely have been there, especially with everything that was going on with the job. I couldn't bring anyone else into that madness until things changed. It was either her or me. I had already told HR I was looking outside the hospital to plan my exit. Basically, they looked at her record and then looked at mine and asked me what they could do to assist me to stay."

This time I turned to her with shock on my face. Nat's record must've been impressive for the hospital to respond like that. Just then, Mom and Dad walked to the door, announcing themselves. In hindsight, I was glad they did. I had several guns in the house, and I knew how to use them. I'd gotten them right after I filed for divorce and after I moved out of the house we shared.

"Hey, Mr. and Mrs. Greene, how are you guys?" Natalie asked as she turned around on the sofa to face them.

"Oh, we are fine, darling. How have you been?" Marjorie asked.

"I'm doing good, Mrs. Greene."

"Toni, we're going upstairs to enjoy the television so we won't disturb your conversation."

"Okay."

I locked the door behind them while watching them both walk up the stairs hand in hand. I swear they were still mesmerized by each other like they were when they had us,

I thought to myself.

"These dating profiles are nothing more than the person's representative."

"I know, and the guy I met last night, Toni, was everything I hoped he was. We're going to go out again after Christmas, and he wants to have kids and settle down."

"I just hope you also take it slow, Nat. I mean, you're my girl, and I don't want to see you get hurt or misled."

"Same for you, Toni. I don't want to see you get hurt. So what are you going to do with Paul if Eric says he wants to get serious?"

"I already told Paul it would be best if we were to be friends and see how things progressed from there. As far as Eric goes, I don't know, but I know him and I have a lot to discuss when he comes to see me."

"Okay, keep me posted. I'm going to leave and go home and take a nice long bath. This shift was particularly brutal with us being short-staffed since the holidays are around the corner."

"Okay, well, look, if you are able to leave out early on Christmas Day, you are always welcome to swing by and have dinner with us."

I invited her because I knew her family wasn't visiting, and she hadn't mentioned anything about going home to see them this year. Usually, when she was off for Christmas or Thanksgiving, she would travel to Florida to see them.

"I will be sure to keep that in mind. Thank you for listening, Toni. I may stop by the package store and get something for home."

"Okay, Nat, don't party too hard now." We walked to the door together, hugged, and she was out the door. I went upstairs to see if Mom and Dad were ready for dinner since they hadn't come down to get something to eat. I knocked on the bedroom door and asked if they were getting something to eat or if Mom was cooking.

"You can cook something, Toni. Also, since tomorrow is Christmas Eve, may as well take the food out of the deep freezer and place it in the refrigerator."

Mom was so good at giving directions. I smiled to myself. I walked down the stairs heading toward the kitchen. As I started cooking dinner, I received a text from Eric. "Hi, Toni, we are still on for next week. I just confirmed the hotel booking for the downtown Houston area. I am really looking forward to seeing you again." I texted back that I was looking forward to seeing him again. He texted that he would fly in on the 29th and would text me once he got settled in at the hotel. Sweet, I thought to myself.

I walked over to the deep freezer and took out the ham and rolls and greens. Once I put all of that in the refrigerator, I finished up cooking dinner. Since it was so hot outside, I decided to make chicken salad. After I finished that part, I put it in the fridge to get a slight chill. Mom and Dad came into the kitchen, sitting at the table.

"I'm just waiting for the chicken salad to get cold," I told them.

I started on a nice salad and served that until the other part of the dinner was ready.

T'IS THE SEASON

The next day was Christmas Eve. This year seemed to fast forward by. Trish and Leon had arrived last night and checked into a hotel. Kevin texted me this morning and said he and Donte were arriving later in the morning. Dee called Mom and told her they'd be here in time for dinner. I thought to myself, everyone is where they're supposed to be. I'd taken a shower and got dressed and, of course, heard my parents talking amongst each other as I went downstairs into the kitchen.

"Toni, can you take out the ham or make sure it has thawed out?" Mom asked.

I went into the refrigerator and felt around the huge ham and said I thought it was thawed enough to place in the oven.

"Okay, good," Mom said while getting up and turning the oven on.

"Do you guys want some of the leftover breakfast casserole? I can throw that in the oven."

"Sounds good to me," Dad chimed in.

I took the casserole out and placed it in the oven. I put the timer on, and while that was happening, I started on the string beans for dinner. Mom had the coffee percolating in the coffee machine.

"Toni, that coffee smells so good. You'll have to tell me the brand so I can pick up some once we get back to Carolina."

"Will do, Mom."

The traditional Christmas dinner consisted of ham, string beans, rolls, macaroni and cheese, any variety of cake, and apple pie. Our dinner was smaller in scale compared to the Thanksgiving feast. I heard the doorbell ring as I was pulling the casserole out of the oven.

"I'll get it," Dad said, proceeding to walk toward the front door.

I peeked out from the kitchen, and it was Trish and her family. I spoke as they piled into the living room. Trish looked tired as she walked into the kitchen.

"Is that the breakfast casserole on the counter?"

"Yep, it sure is," I said as I turned back around to put the ham into the oven.

"Trish, are you okay?" I asked as she walked to the table and sat down.

"Yeah, girl, we got up early to catch this flight in, and I'm feeling the effects of it."

I thought to myself, they must've had a long night too and didn't want to say anything in front of our parents.

"Yeah, oh, okay," I said and sat down at the table and started eating.

I was glad they did come back for Christmas. I'd had my assistant go shopping while I was in Bora Bora. I hoped she was able to find everything I put on the list. All I saw under the tree was a pile of presents. I'd looked through them a couple of days ago, and they were labeled. I tried to get the kids at least what they wanted, but as for my siblings and their husbands, gift cards all the way. I did have some making up to do, though, not being able to celebrate the holidays around them for several years. I just hoped everyone was happy with the gifts.

"Is Dee coming by herself?" Trish asked.

"Yeah, her and the kids."

"Oh, okay. How are they doing, by the way?"

"They seem to be working the situation out in therapy. Dee sounded like she was hopeful the last time I spoke to her."

I could only speculate if she was actually happy with the process or if Tim was trying to work on getting past her cheating. Either way, I was glad to see her and the kids when she got here. Then, of course, we'd know the full story.

"I'm going upstairs to take a much-deserved shower and change my clothes," Trish said, getting up from the table. "We only went to the hotel to put our luggage in the rooms and take some bathroom breaks. The kids had time to get themselves together before the flight. Leon and I skipped that part since it would've just made us late arriving at the airport."

"Hey, I understand. The last thing you want is to hold up the airplane schedule," I said.

She and Leon had packed a small bag of clothes after they got to the hotel suite and decided to shower at my house. I got it—that was the only thing I didn't like about traveling. The airplane bathrooms were a joke, and if you did decide to use them, there was always someone holding up the bathroom, doing whatever. I turned to Mom and asked her if she'd spoken to Dee. She shook her head that she hadn't. I texted Dee and asked her what time she was arriving into the airport and if she had a way to get to the house. Nothing. I hoped she was okay with her and the kids traveling alone.

"I haven't received a reply back yet, Mom. Hopefully she's en route on the airplane."

Mom nodded and got up to start on the rolls. I left the kitchen and went upstairs to check on Trish and her husband. The kids were all in the living room looking at some new game on YouTube that was about to come out. I shook my head, thinking to myself, they'd be asking their dad for another game that they might play thirty minutes at the most. Once I arrived upstairs, I peered into one of the bedrooms, and there were Leon and Trish, both sound asleep. Yeah, early flight, alright—more like bedroom antics before an early flight. I then laughed to myself. They were both in a deep sleep.

I then walked into my bedroom and checked on some emails to see what clients were interested in what houses. I then walked back downstairs and joined the kids on the sofa. Mom was busy doing her thing in the kitchen, and Dad had gone out for a walk around the neighborhood. They were looking at all the new games coming out for the next year. I asked them out of all the games, which one they'd really like to play. The funny thing was, only two of the girls were gamers like that. The oldest, Tasha, was only looking to be nosy. Timeka and Tara both said they liked the new simulation game that was coming out. Tara played a lot of simulation games and racing games. Timeka played first-person shooter games. I made a mental note of which games they were eyeing closely.

I was thinking of getting them for each of their birthdays, but I wanted to run that by their parents first.

Dee just responded back that she and the kids had landed and were renting a car.

"Mom, Dee and the kids are on their way," I yelled into the kitchen.

"Okay," she said.

Dee also texted that Tim decided to just stay at the house. Hmm, interesting, I thought to myself. She said they were going to the hotel to relax for a bit and then head over here. I texted her back that that sounded good and I'd see her when she got here. I went into the kitchen to help Mom set up the food on the counter. I got a text message from Paul wishing me a Merry Christmas, and then shortly after, Eric wished me a Merry Christmas. I decided to call Eric and see how he was celebrating the holidays. He, of course, said he was excited to see me and the holidays were okay. He was visiting his family and sorting out their drama that had transpired over an Uno game. Yep, you read that right. Any card games could pop off family drama depending on who was doing the cheating within the game. His family appeared to be no different.

Our family didn't play cards like that. We mostly played board games, so we avoided the family arguments that came with that. However, we'd played Uno a few times. We set the rules in the game at the beginning, and they weren't complex rules like reverse Uno or stacking. I told him I hoped he was being the peacemaker and not the instigator. He laughed and said he wasn't even involved. I found that hard to believe because Eric in college made it his business to clown whoever couldn't play the game correctly. I remembered him having a black eye in college because one of those games had gotten out of hand. So him not having anything to do with this one was suspicious. He could have changed since college, though, so I did try to give him the benefit of the doubt. I told him I was excited to see him and looking forward to the date. After we hung up, I thought to myself, I just wanted to feel him in my arms.

Getting back to the food, the setup was almost done. The ham looked nice and glazed. It was about the same size as the one that was done during Thanksgiving. By this time, Dad came into the kitchen checking over everything. Tara and Timeka both came into the kitchen, smelling the aroma of the food from the living room. I told them we were going to eat in about another thirty minutes or so. Then Trish walked into the kitchen and told the girls to go and wash their hands. Trish looked well rested this time.

"Uh-huh, I peeped on you two earlier. You were so sound asleep, I don't think you heard the door open," I said while slightly smiling.

"Yeah," then Trish came closer to me to whisper in my ear, "you know Leon wanted to have sex since the girls were already asleep, which gave us time alone," she said barely above a whisper.

"Well, I kind of put two and two together because just being tired from the plane ride was not it," I laughed lower this time.

She laughed back and shook her head. I then proceeded to take the remainder of the breakfast casserole and threw it in the trash. Besides Christmas morning, I planned on making pancakes and bacon. Leon was in the living room while Tasha talked to him about her next year's birthday gift.

Mom asked everyone to gather around the kitchen table for a quick grace. Everyone gathered around to say grace and then began to pass around the food and plates. Leon was cutting the ham a little deeper even though it was pre-cut. I'd sent out several Merry Christmas messages to my associates, friends, and staff. I'd already sent out cards to their respective residences.

I heard the doorbell ring as Mom was finishing up grace. I knew it was Kevin. He'd texted earlier that he was going to be later than expected. I walked over to the door and opened it. Kevin and his son walked in, and we all exchanged hugs.

"Come on into the kitchen. We've started eating already," I said.

Timeka and Tara both hugged their cousin. Then they started showing him the new releases for the coming year. Kevin walked into the kitchen behind me, and Trish got up to give him a hug. I sat back down to finish my food. I was looking forward to Mom's lemon pound cake this time around.

"Hey, everyone," Kevin's voice bellowed throughout the kitchen.

He and his son gathered around at the table and sat down to grab some of the food. I swear when my brother makes a plate, he knows how to make a plate! I was still astonished at how much he ate and seemed to maintain a good physique. Mom got up and walked over to the fridge to get out the dessert. She was so excited because she hadn't baked dessert in a long time. Besides, we were all watching our waistlines these days and trying to eat on the healthier side.

The doorbell rang, and I got up to get it again. This time it was Dee and her kids.

"Hey, Toni," she said as she and the kids walked through the door.

She looked stressed and tired. The kids immediately smelled the food and flowed into the kitchen. As I shut the door behind me, Dee stated she needed to talk to me.

"Things are going okay at home, but Tim said he 'needed space' away from us," she said while using air quotes at the same time.

"Dee, all I can say is it's going to take time, and right now you're really still in the rough patch."

"I know, Toni, but I'm forever feeling punished for making one mistake."

We talked in the living room for a while amongst each other.

"I'm feeling stressed, tired, and I've started saving and paying off as much as I can. I don't want to be blindsided by a divorce, Toni."

Understandably, she had every right to feel the way she felt, and I could sort of empathize with her, but I was more sympathetic to Tim. I'd been the person betrayed, left out in the cold—or rather the person on the outside looking in on the so-called relationship. At least she was given time to save and pay off bills just in case he decided to walk away. I wasn't given that choice, and it was beyond an embarrassment to have to ask my parents for a loan in their elder years. Nope, my lovely ex decided one day he was done with me and the marriage. He didn't even look back. He said in the letter to me HIS happiness was more important than living with an obnoxious, self-righteous know-it-all. The name-calling, of course, was a deflection from the real issue.

I was in denial, and he was gaslighting me. Adding

to my already low self-esteem only gave me ammunition for my lawyer.

"Dee, I know you're going through it, and you know the door is always open to you and the children whenever you guys need a break from each other," I offered, as it was the least I could do in that situation.

"I know, sis, but I am so tired mentally of having to play on the defense instead of the offense. I want, for once, for him to forget I ever slept with anybody else!" This time Dee was angry. "No, he doesn't see what he did or didn't do as warranted of me having stepped outside of the marriage," she continued. "Toni, I was miserable and missing the physical, mental, and emotional connection."

"Dee, why didn't you convince Tim at that time to go to the therapist as a family? I'm not judging, but that should've been the last resort, not the first option. It really shouldn't be an option at all, though," I said with shrugged shoulders.

I didn't know what Dee wanted from me on this topic. I couldn't judge her reasons, but I also couldn't cosign that what she did was right. It wasn't.

"Toni, in the early part of the marriage, we started having problems after I had Brittani," she continued. "I tried many times to tell Tim that something wasn't right between us, but he kept chalking it up to postpartum depression. He never listened to me when I told him, no, this is something different. The distance between us—I noticed it, and he said it was because he was working and his caseload had become really heavy."

Hearing this, I asked Dee, "So when that happened, did you do a surprise pop-up at the job to see if that was what was going on?" I asked, genuinely curious.

"Yes, and he was there working like he said, and sometimes he would welcome the break in the work pace, but sometimes he had a tone that he didn't appreciate me being there unannounced," she said.

"Okay, then obviously that was a miscommunication somewhere between the two of you," I told her that as long as she didn't suspect anything wrong, then she should have told him it seemed there was a distance here, and it wasn't because she'd just had the baby. I told her men and women managed stressful situations differently, and talking that out would have cleared the air between them instead of just pushing the issue under the rug and hoping it would fix itself.

By this time, Trish and Leon came into the living room and asked Dee if she wanted to eat something. Their welcome break gave me a chance to regroup from the draining conversation. I loved my sister Dee with all my heart, but the constant avoidance of taking accountability on her part was not what she was ready to hear at this moment. After she got to the point of taking some ownership of this, then she could really begin to heal. I'd had to do the same thing with my marriage. I knew the red flags were there, and I'd only called my ex out on a few of them, but as he became more conniving with his lies, I just mentally got to a point where I'd excuse them. That was also part of seeking help with therapy.

"Trish, I'm going to grab some dessert," I said as I got up and walked into the kitchen.

Dad and Mom decided to go for a walk to let some of the food settle. I cleared the empty plates from the table and asked my brother if he had any prospects for the new year coming in.

"Toni, I've been on several dating sites, but I think my expectations with women must be high."

"Oh, why do you say that?" I asked.

"There were a few that I was interested in, so I went on a coffee date with them just to see where their head was at."

Just then, Donte was asking to be excused as he and his cousin Curt wanted to go upstairs and play on one of the gaming systems.

"We'll come with you too," Brittani chimed in, and then Tara, Timeka, and Tasha all followed upstairs.

"Well, that's one way to clear the room out, Kevin," I said jokingly.

Laughing, he said, "I know. Talking about our personal lives makes these children cringe, like we don't deserve to date or anything. Anyway, well, the one sister I took out, she wanted, first of all, a fee to see how serious I was about asking her on a date," he continued. "Another wanted to live chat first to make sure my picture matched what I looked like in person. I told her, 'You do know people can use a filter or AI to throw off how they really look, but okay.' Then another one wanted the same as the first one, but she was bolder with it. She said, 'You need to take me to a five-star restaurant for a first date,' emphasizing that she does not do coffee dates."

I was really taken aback. Had the dating pool gotten that—dare I say—money-hungry and opportunistic?

"My, my, that sounds crazy," I shook my head in disbelief.

I did know my brother well, though, and I knew he had high standards, and I also knew he tended to try to go for the physically appealing woman versus the beauty-and-brains type.

"But," he said, "I did meet someone that we have the same common interests, and I'm taking this slow."

"Oh, good. I have hope for you to find love, Kevin."

"So far this one, she's special, and I like how we just get each other."

Both of us were trying to stay positive in finding love. His son's mom, Chrissy, liked the idea of having a baby with Kevin but didn't consider how much responsibility it took to raise a child.

"I'm trying to stay positive, Kev," I said, which was true. I wanted nothing but good intentions for both me and my brother. We'd both been through crazy situations.

"Me too, sis. Me too," he said as he got up from the table and told me he'd do the dishes this time.

Trish and Leon were both in the other room talking to Dee. She did end up getting something to eat, but I knew she didn't have much appetite with everything going on. I peeked out from the kitchen at them and thought to myself, Dee was lucky she had the support system around her. Thinking back to the situation I was in, I'd had to lean on the friends I had. Thankfully, they rallied around me and gave me the courage to move on after Christian left. He told me after the fact that he'd sold the house. I saw the for-sale sign and knew I had only a couple of days to get my things packed. I'd had to be there to walk prospective clients through the house. He literally left everything to fall on me. Then had the nerve to tell me what price he was willing to take for the house and nothing less. "I had to make it work," he said. Of course, in his greed, he'd skipped on some regular maintenance with the house, and I'd had to make sure the HVAC system was up to date. I'd had to make sure the lawn care was done and that the pool was cleaned out and maintained, all while I had to look for a new place to stay. Cold-hearted, to say the least.

Finding out he'd stopped paying the mortgage three months before the house was being sold was really cruel. I'd had to advise the mortgage company when the house was being closed to stop them from starting the foreclosure process. He, of course, didn't tell them anything—just stopped paying. I was more excited for the house to sell than anyone because I'd had to immediately pay two months of mortgage and had almost gone into the negative in my savings account. I wasn't about to pay them from my business account. All Christian said when I told him was, "I know you had it, so you took care of it." Argh!! Frustrating and angry at the same time. There were some lines I didn't cross, even if the person hurt me or vice versa. I would never do that to Christian. Matter of fact, his parents would've tracked me down and read me the riot act for leaving their precious son in a precarious situation. I didn't tell my parents any of this until after the fact, when the divorce was getting closer to being finalized. Dad was pissed, and the younger him would've definitely tracked Christian down and handled business. So when I said I was trying to stay positive for Kevin and me, it was definitely warranted in both cases.

Snapping out of my thoughts, Dee and Trish walked into the kitchen, still talking. Leon, I noticed, went upstairs at some point in the conversation, and our parents had come back from walking. The children were upstairs still playing games. They could play on the consoles for hours.

"Dee, give it a rest," Trish said. "I know you want to get your point across, but this time you're in the wrong," Trish continued. "I told her this," I nodded in agreement.

"It seems you're not taking ownership in this situation," Trish said. "Do you not see that if you didn't sleep with someone, this whole situation could have been avoided? Now, sis, normally I will have your back on what issues you're going through, but not on this."

Trish looked at me and then at Dee.

"Dee, no, you were in the wrong by doing it at all," Trish adamantly said.

I just stood there waiting for Dee to have a comeback to defend her actions. She didn't. Instead, she walked around and went outside for some air. I looked at Trish.

"I walked in the kitchen for a reason after talking to Dee. She still thinks what she did is justification for not being treated right."

"Right. I know because Leon and I were hearing a little bit of what she was telling you from the kitchen, so we both were shaking our heads in disbelief. Then she tried to pull the same thing with both of us, and Leon walked away, and I knew he was getting upset about what she was saying."

Trish walked over to the table and cut some of the cake.

"I know, Trish. When Dee is like this, there's no getting through to her," I said. "She's going to continue to think she's right even though she had time to discuss this with Tim way before it had gotten to that point," I continued. "She's not ready yet, and I think even the therapist knows that."

Mom walked into the kitchen, overhearing what we were talking about, and said to us, "I know Dee doesn't want to hear what you guys are saying because she hasn't accepted the fact that she messed up. Until that happens—and I know my child—she is very stubborn, and she wants you guys to agree that what she did was right."

All three of us nodded in agreement. That's what this was about. It was that we weren't having her back, and instead we were siding with Tim. She was seeing us as the enemy that wasn't cosigning on her foolishness.

"Mom, I appreciate you confirming that we're right in this situation."

"Let me tell you something," she said. "You all are grown adults, and I have to live with the decisions each of you make in your lives every day, and I have to know when to guide you with advice but at the same time learn to back off and let you make your own decisions."

Mom brought her wisdom into the conversation.

"Your father told me a long time ago that when you guys get married, do not intervene in the marriage. He said that will only push them away from you and that it will backfire always. He said that was what his mom told him when he married me. His mom and I got along great, and I couldn't ask for a better mother-in-law who was not trying to compete with me," Mom continued as she looked between me and Trish. "His mom told me, 'I know my son loves you, but if you two run into any trouble, I'm staying out of it, respectfully.' That was the most valuable thing I learned from my mother-in-law that day going forward. This means that Dee and Tim will need to focus on each other to make it through this. I know you all are trying to help, but this is where we need to all move on and let them work on it themselves."

That was the truth, but all of us knew it hurt to see Dee go through this.

"I did the same thing with you, Toni. I told you to figure it out if you wanted to stay married, but I didn't think he wanted to stay, and you can't make someone do anything they don't want to do."

"Yeah, I remember," I chimed in and said, "I knew you wanted only the best for me by not holding my hand and taking over the situation."

"Right. Toni, what did I tell you that day you wanted advice?"

"You said, 'Figure it out, baby girl.'"

"Exactly," Mom said.

"I did eventually, and I know I made the right choice. I won't downplay that it didn't hurt when he left, but I slowly had gotten my self-esteem back and went to a therapist to figure the rest out."

"Trish came to me a few times, and I told her you need to talk to your husband."

Trish nodded in agreement.

"So it's not just you, Toni, but all of you have come to me about this or that situation with the marriage, and I told you respectfully that you need to figure it out. Was it hard doing that? Of course it was!" Mom said and then got up to see what Dad was up to.

I knew from then on to have nothing but respect for my mom. In my eyes, that took a strong person to say, "Hey, you have to handle this on your own" or "This situation is just temporary." The same for Dee, but it was going to take her more time to willingly admit to her hand in what she was going through. As Kevin was doing the dishes, he was listening and looking on in disbelief because the mom he knew handled him a little differently. He knew he was definitely the young one of the family, and Mom was not going to coddle him either. Dad was different when it came to him and still gave him the respect to make his own decisions. After Kevin had made several questionable decisions, Dad took him under his wing and guided him. I knew for a fact my brother wouldn't have gotten as far in his career and social circle if our dad hadn't shown him a better way of addressing certain situations.

I glanced down and Nat was calling my cell phone.

"Hey, lady," I said into the phone.

Natalie was doing a countdown about Eric coming to visit worse than I was. She asked all kinds of questions—where were we eating, did I already have the outfits picked out to wear, and how long was he staying in town? I reassured her that I'd already picked out what to wear, including the lingerie, and he'd already picked the restaurant, and as far as I knew, he was staying only for the weekend.

"Nat, we're just taking this time to get to know each other again. He's not staying for the week, and we've not seen each other in at least ten years."

Nat definitely led with her heart on her sleeve. I loved her like my own siblings, but throughout the years, she'd definitely had up-and-down relationships. I had hope she'd find someone who would pour into her like she'd poured into her past relationships. Hanging up the phone, I got up to find out where Dee went. Dad said something about her going for a walk to clear her mind. I went out the front door and started dialing her number to see how far she was from the house.

"Yes," Dee answered the phone.

"Hey, just checking to see where you are so I can walk over to you and talk," I said.

She'd actually made it quite far from the house, so I started walking to catch up to her. As I walked to where she was seated, I noticed she had this sad look on her face.

"Okay, I'm here. So what did you want to talk about, Toni?" she looked at me through sad eyes.

"I just want to check on you and if this walk worked in clearing your mind from the conversations that were had earlier."

"Well, my mind is made up if that's what you want to know," she said with a concerned look on her face.

"So once you get back home, what are you going to do?" I asked honestly.

"I decided until Tim and I get to a place where therapy is starting to help, I'm going to move out of the house for a while."

"Hmm, that's not what I expected you to say, but I respect your decision," I said.

"Please don't tell anyone, Toni. Keep this between us."

She confided in me more about why she felt she needed space in the marriage and away from the children. She felt that Tim didn't really participate in the sessions with the therapist, and she felt like he wasn't really wanting to work on the marriage.

"I don't think he can get past what I did, Toni. I think he really wants a divorce. He told you guys that he went to his parents for Christmas, but I really think he went on another trip. I haven't been able to reach him since he supposedly left for his parents' house. The kids are asking me all the time why they can't reach their dad, and I really don't have the answer for that."

She started tearing up a bit, and I reached around and put my arm on her shoulder.

"Listen, whatever he's doing or not doing, I know it's going to work out for the best," I continued. "If that means divorce or taking a long break to figure out what you want and what he wants, it will work out."

I tried to reassure her that no matter what, family would stand behind her. I let her cry it out and lean into me because she needed me to be there, and I wanted to. I hadn't been there before, and I wanted to make up for the lost time, especially in this situation. We both got up and started walking back toward the house.

"Thank you," she replied in a low whisper-like tone.

I knew she needed that, and it didn't take us too long to get back to the house. When we both walked through the door, Trish was staring at us both. Neither Dee nor I said anything. We both needed something sweet to soothe the pain of what she had to decide. Mom's pound cake came in handy. Maybe Mom knew this conversation would take place and made the cake. Trish walked into the kitchen with us and sat down as we both cut a piece of cake.

"So, Dee, how was the walk?" Trish asked.

"It was good, Trish. I got to mentally zone out and then make a list in my mind of what the next steps with my marriage would look like."

Dee said nothing further on the subject and instead focused on eating the cake.

"This cake I have so missed. It is delicious," Dee said, changing the subject.

"It sure is. I agree. I forgot how good Mom's cakes are."

I didn't want to even get into more of what Trish wanted to ask Dee.

"So we're just going to brush over the fact that I want to know more details about the next steps?" Trish asked, looking at Dee with an intensity in her eyes.

"Oh, you may want to know more, but I'm not going to talk about it anymore," Dee stood firm.

"Okay," was all Trish would say.

She got up and started putting away the food from the dinner earlier. Trish deep down knew once Dee's mind was made up on not discussing something, there was no way to change it. The rest of the time the family was here went in a blur. Trish and her family flew back the next day after Christmas. Mom and Dad left two days later along with Dee and the kids. By Friday, I had the house to myself, and it felt rather strange.

Layla had come over and helped me take down the Christmas decorations inside and outside of the house. I really appreciated her helping because I was two seconds from hiring somebody to take all of these decorations down.

"Layla, how have you been?" I asked while she was taking the ornaments off of the tree.

"I've been good. Christmas and Thanksgiving were good. We went to Chris's parents' home for Thanksgiving and went to my parents' house for Christmas."

I nodded as she was talking. Chris was her boyfriend, but I thought it was about to get serious now that they were spending time with each other's families.

"That's really good, and you know the fam came out to see me, and I kind of miss them slightly, maybe a little bit now that they're gone," I confessed.

"Yes, I know you do, and if they were closer, you probably wouldn't miss them as much," she said in agreement.

"Yeah, I know. I tried to get my parents to move this way so they don't have to fly all the time. They could just drive, but they were not entertaining that," I said. "I think the heat in Texas has a lot to do with their decision, though."

"So if given the chance, would you move closer to them?" she asked.

"You know, I have been thinking about that or at least being open to it," I said.

We spent another hour finishing up taking the decorations down, and then she asked if I needed anything. I told her no, I was good, and to have a good weekend. After closing the door, I started putting the decorations into the storage closet and then put the outside decorations in the garage. I was so glad at the time I'd invested in the storage bins for all these decorations. After all of that, I sat on the sofa in the living room and started channel surfing, trying to find a good movie. I heard my phone chime a few times and looked down to see there were several text messages from Eric. He confirmed he'd be arriving Saturday morning around ten AM. Once he settled into the hotel room, he'd call me and confirm what time I wanted to go out for lunch. I texted him back that I was looking forward to seeing hixm.

I went back to looking at the television for what seemed like several hours and realized I must have nodded off. I got up feeling like I had a hangover and went to check the front door and sliding door to make sure they were locked and the alarm had been set. I then walked up the stairs, realizing I hadn't heard any conversations or young people's voices in the house. Man, this feels really lonely now, I thought to myself. I slammed into the bed after getting undressed. My mind, of course, went to the upcoming evening planned with Eric. Oh, I can't wait to feel those arms around me, I thought to myself as I began to drift off to sleep.

A Toast to Real Friendship

The next morning I woke up refreshed as I heard the birds chirping outside the windows. I knew exactly what dress I was going to wear today and the outfit for tonight. After sitting up in bed for some time, I jumped into the shower and thought about the dress. It was a strapless pink dress that hit in all the right places. I'd worn it before and gotten a ton of compliments on it. I had some nice heels to go with it, not too high and not too low. I got out of the shower and put on some lotion, then threw on some clothes and lounged around the house until it was time to meet Eric.

My phone rang, and I had to check the time because I knew only a few people would call me this early in the morning. It was Trish.

"Hi, Trish, and good morning," I said into the phone.

She began to ask me about the date coming up.

"You are almost as bad as Natalie. Nat had a million questions, and so do you, I see," she laughed, and I began to laugh too.

"Well, you know it's been so long, girl, and if anybody can blow your back out, it's him," she said, and I immediately blushed.

"Trish, stop it," I started laughing as soon as she said it. She had no filter.

"You know it's the truth. Stop being in denial."

I cracked up some more.

"I have to get some breakfast in my stomach, woman, so I've got to go," I said and hung up the phone, but not before telling her I loved her and the family.

That sister of mine was sometimes a real mess. I thought about what she said, and Trish might be funny, but she never told a lie. Whew, I thought to myself. She was absolutely right. Eric was like my yang to his yin. Sex had always been explosive with us, and I secretly wished I'd ended up marrying him instead of Christian. I was sure we would have had at least three kids by now. He really was crushing on me in college, but my mind was somewhere else and with someone else. Christian, when I met him, had the dreamy looks and potential to be anything he put his mind to.

Wiping that memory away, I started eating and had my morning coffee. The time was going so fast—it was already ten o'clock, and right on cue, my phone rang. It was Eric.

"Hello there," I said into the phone.

"Well, I know that voice anywhere. How are you?" he asked.

His voice hadn't changed one bit since college. It almost melted my soul when he spoke.

"I've been doing well for myself," I said and then told him, "I'm looking forward to seeing you again after all this time."

"Yes, definitely. So I just got everything unpacked at the place I'm staying at. What time would you want to meet up?" he inquired.

"One o'clock would be good for me," I said.

"Okay, that'll work for me as it gives me time to get ready and put away my things," he agreed. "I'm going to text you the address of where to meet me."

I said okay and then told him I'd see him soon. Hanging up the phone, three seconds later I received the address to the restaurant. Oh, that's not too far from here, I thought to myself. I started getting ready and made sure I had everything I needed in case I was going back to the place where he was staying. Back in the day, I always had what some people would call a spend-the-night bag. That way, if you wanted to stay with someone, you wouldn't have to rush home to get any change of clothes or endure the walk of shame from not having said clothes.

I decided to use Waze for the GPS to the restaurant. I put everything in the overnight bag and made sure to lock the door on the way out to the car. It would take me about twenty minutes to get to the restaurant, which wasn't bad in traffic around here. I arrived at the restaurant and parked the car. I'd decided to go with a nice red sundress with the arms out and the dress falling right below the knees. I got out of the car and walked toward the door of the restaurant. I felt a sudden chill as I was walking, even though it was hot out. I quickly scanned the parking lot and brushed off the feeling.

As I got to the waitress, I told her two people would be at the table. She said a person was here waiting for me. As I scanned the room, I saw him waving me over. I thought to myself, oh my goodness. He really hasn't changed much since college—still mocha smooth. He had a bit more weight on the stomach area, no washboard abs from what I could tell, but the few extra pounds made him even sexier than I remembered. There he sat in a nice white short-sleeve shirt and brown khaki pants, still with that irresistible smile.

"Hi," he said as I sat down.

"Hi," I said back, and all those memories came flooding in big time.

It felt like time had stopped when we looked across at each other.

"You still look beautiful," he said to me, and of course I started blushing.

"Thank you," was all I could muster as I became locked in on how good he looked.

"I see you still looking sexy as ever," I said while taking in every inch of his physical presence.

"I miss you now that you're sitting here in front of me," he confessed. "I haven't been doing too much lately besides now being a sports agent and in the process of opening up my own business."

"Okay, and how is that going?" I asked.

"It has its challenges, but I'm so excited to pursue this avenue," he said while looking at me with those intense brown eyes of his.

I could get lost in his eyes.

"So have you been here before?" he inquired.

"I haven't, and I've traveled much of the city. I like the atmosphere here. It's really relaxed, and the music is a good selection," I added.

"You're in real estate now. How is that going?"

"It also has its moments, but seeing clients happy is really what motivates me. Sometimes it's the day-to-day administrative part that I have to deal with that can be challenging."

"Well, with much success comes much requirement," he said.

We then ordered our drinks and food when the waiter reappeared.

"I see you haven't changed much after college physically, but you seem to have changed mentally," I said while taking a sip on the red wine I'd ordered.

"You know, at some point, maturity comes into play, and a lot of my past relationships taught me to bring the emotional connection necessary to maintain those relationships," he confessed. "The reason my marriage didn't work out was both of us needed work emotionally, physically, and mentally. I own up to what my part was in the marriage, but I had two beautiful kids, and I wouldn't change anything about that part," he continued. "I had to realize in order to go to the next level, I had to take a break and work on myself. Me and my former wife were good as friends but not so good in a marriage. I'm not going to lie, Toni, when I reached out to your sister, I was definitely hoping you weren't married anymore and secretly wanting to start over again with us," he admitted.

I sat there for a moment, stunned, because deep down I was hoping he'd say that. We'd definitely both matured and were different people than we were in college, but we still had chemistry between each other. I felt the same way. I wanted a chance at us to start over, and who knew where this would go.

"I have to be upfront with you, Eric. If we start again, I'd have to take it slow," I continued. "My marriage messed me up emotionally, physically, and mentally. The gaslighting in the end, the love bombing in the beginning, and the abuse in between. I've healed from that through continuous therapy and finding peace through meditation."

I looked in his eyes for any sign of deception and didn't see any. He might be ready to bring me the love I needed and deserved.

"I had to learn how to love myself again, Eric. I had to learn how to build my self-esteem back up, and that's what gave me the confidence to leave the marriage. I had a support system between friends until I was able to have my family back in my life again."

Eric nodded as I told him about what transpired with me since leaving college.

"I'm at a place, Eric, where I'm open to love again," I said. Life was one big roller coaster, and there were no guarantees of seeing another day.

"Well, that's good to hear because I was hoping you'd say that. I'm going to take it as slow as you want to. Reconnecting as friends is the important part. Are you okay with that?" he asked.

"I am."

We sat around for several more hours just catching up and realized it was getting late.

"If you don't have any plans tomorrow, I'd like to take you out for dinner," he said.

"That sounds good," I said, getting up, and he reached out toward me and got up to give me a hug.

He felt so good that I got lost in the hug. He must've felt it too because after that, he asked to walk me to my car. Once we got to the car, I turned to him, and we kissed each other. It wasn't planned, but things were always easy between him and me. When we kissed, I instantly felt the familiar sparks between our lips. The kiss felt like it lasted forever. We both needed this kiss. It felt like the world stopped spinning as we played with each other's tongues. It was just the right amount of tongue, not too overwhelming and sloppy. Here I was, getting lost in the feeling, when I felt him pulling back. We both just looked at each other. It felt like ten years hadn't gone by, like we were right back in college. We both grinned at each other, and then he asked if I wanted to go back to the hotel he was staying at. I agreed. He, of course, reiterated that if I wasn't ready to take that step, he'd be okay with it. He said he'd cry on the inside but respected my position. I assured him I was ready, that after ten years, I was curious if we still had that chemistry that neither one of us could deny. He said okay.

"Give me a few minutes to get to the car, and if you would follow me there," he said.

Thinking to myself, who was he fooling? That kiss alone got me wetter than I'd ever been with any other guy. As I saw a black SUV pull to the right side of the car, I realized this must be him. That truck was so him. I knew it was a rental, though, since he flew in from California. I began to put the car in reverse to start following him to the hotel. I was nervous, excited, definitely horny all at the same time.

As we approached the hotel, he rolled the driver's side window down and motioned to the area for me to park in. I followed into the parking space, and he parked across from my car. I got out, making sure to grab the bag in the back seat. He met me by the car, and we walked together into the lobby. As we walked in, we made small talk amongst each other. As he unlocked the room, I was a bit taken aback. It was a nice suite, and it had petals and candles everywhere.

"So how do you know I was going to come back here with you?" I asked.

"Oh, just call it intuition," he laughed as he said it, and I had to laugh too.

He knew me too well.

"This looks amazing. It feels good that you put in the effort," I said to him.

Suddenly, he took my bag from my hands and put it in the closet. I then turned around, and he began to undress me. We didn't even have to speak to know what to do to each other next. I had on a nice red bra and panties set with a little lace on each. He stood back and just looked at me. I smiled because I knew what was coming next. He unbuttoned his shirt to reveal a white tank underneath. Then it was my turn to look in amazement. He then turned me around and motioned for me to sit on a chair in the front part of the suite. I did, and then he pulled my arms behind my back and said,

"I know what you want, and I know what you've been missing."

That sent shivers down my spine, and I felt myself getting wetter. In our college days, I used to love when he talked to me, and I used to throw it right back to him.

"You're right. I've missed this, and it's been way too long without it," I agreed.

Then, as he tied my hands at the wrist, I sat in anticipation for the next part. I then felt him taking off my bra and sliding my panties off as I raised up off the chair slightly. He then pulled out the blindfold and tied it around my eyes.

"Now you know it wouldn't be fun for you to look at what I'm doing," he said and then moved me forward almost to the edge of the seat.

He then started feeling my wetness with his fingers, and I could hear him licking them one at a time.

"Mmm, so good," he said.

Then I felt his mouth, and I immediately threw my head back. If tongue game was a tournament, then he'd be one of the winners. The way he licked, sucked, and slurped—I enjoyed every moment of it. I didn't want it to end. He brought me to the edge of orgasm, and I thought to myself I couldn't get enough. Then I felt a combination of pleasure and release rip through me, and he felt it too. He put his tongue in me to lick up the wetness that was now dripping from my body. I climaxed so hard I truly knew I'd squirted a little. He then went around to the back of the chair and untied my hands. Then slowly took off my blindfold. This time he was naked, and I admired looking at his body up and down and the strong nine inches of thickness I knew was waiting for me. He took my hand and ran it from his chest down to his penis. I grabbed it and started rubbing on it. He motioned for me to follow him into the bedroom.

I then climbed onto the bed in the doggy-style position, and he entered me from behind. It had been so long since I'd felt anything that good inside of me. He knew the right way to stroke it and the right pressure and pain to go along with it. I felt him pulsing inside of me, and I started getting wet again. This was what I missed and never had in my marriage. He started spanking me on my butt, and I loved that part. The pain I felt was a good pain. I felt him getting harder and harder, and I responded to all of it. I took my hand and then rubbed my clit gently so I could climax with him. I felt him starting to climax, and I started climaxing at the same time.

"Oh yes, baby, that's it right there. Throw that ass back to me, baby," he said.

"Ohh, ohh, ooooohhh," I said as another orgasm made me feel like I was floating through space.

"Yes, baby, yesssssssss," he said as he climaxed, and I felt him shaking inside of me.

We both collapsed on top of each other, basking in the afterglow. We both shifted so he could hold me in his arms.

"Oh, I needed that," he said as I looked up at him.

"I definitely needed that too," I agreed.

He got up and started blowing out the candles, then jumped back into the bed.

"You felt sooooo good. It was hard not trying to cum too early," he confessed and then said, "I forgot how good that pussy was."

We both laughed.

"Unforgettable," he admitted.

We lay up on each other while he turned on the television. This was the part I really missed. No matter what we both went through, we came together like nothing happened.

"Well, I'm going to jump into the shower. Do you want to join me?" I asked, but it really wasn't a request.

"Yes, I will. Thanks for asking," he said, and we both walked into the bathroom, and I turned on the shower until it was the right temp.

Thankfully, I still had braids in my hair, so I didn't need to grab a shower cap, but I did sweep the braids into a ponytail. Braid hair was way too heavy when wet. He decided to get in first, and I got in front of him after he got his body wet. Both of us grabbed the shower gel and started washing each other. I loved the way his hands felt all over my body. He said,

"I'm not going to lie. I miss this, and I want to get this every day."

Took the thoughts right out of my head, I thought. I nodded, and we both finished up the shower and dried off. I then went into the front part of the suite and grabbed the clothes I'd packed and started putting them on. I noticed Eric staring at me, and I instantly looked up.

"I can't stop staring at you," he said.

He was also getting dressed, and he went toward me and started kissing me again.

"We cannot get back into the bed again," I said.

"I agree. I'm going to do some looking around in this nice city, and I look forward to seeing you at dinner tomorrow."

He walked back into the bedroom area and started watching the local news.

"I look forward to our dinner as well."

I walked over and bent down to give him a kiss. I turned around, grabbed my bag, and walked over toward the door. I was still feeling like I was walking on air from the sex earlier. It had gotten noticeably darker outside, and I got into the car to head home. Good thoughts filled my mind, and I liked the feeling of it.

As I walked into the living room, I looked around at remnants of my family visit. I saw Tara left her headphones, Dee left a sweater I was sure she thought she'd packed, and my parents left a note I hadn't noticed before. I picked up the note and started reading it. "We are so proud to call you our daughter. You could've let that marriage destroy you, but it didn't. He was determined to take away your spirit, but you are still here. We want nothing but the best for you, dear. Signed, Mom and Dad."

Tears began to swell up in my eyes because I secretly hoped they had my back and were in my corner. During the whole ordeal, I knew it was hard for them to watch me suffer from the sidelines. At the end of the day, they'd do anything for any one of their children, and I was no exception. I decided to call Mom and let her know I'd read the note they left.

"Mom, thank you so much for this," I said into the phone.

"Baby, I'm glad you read it. At first we didn't know where to leave it for you to be able to find it, so we decided to just place it on the table. We knew you'd find it at the right moment. We love you, dear, and don't you forget it."

"I love you both. Take care," I said as I ended the call.

My phone rang again, and this time it was Natalie. I knew she had lots of questions about Eric and my date and wanted all the details.

"What's up, Nat?" I spoke into the phone.

"Girl, so how did it go? Tell me everything," she yelled into the phone.

"Okay, so the lunch date couldn't have gone any better. It was like we didn't miss a beat, Nat. We talked a long time, and he admitted he wanted to give us another try."

"Yesssss," she screamed into the phone.

I knew that would be her reaction. She'd always been a fan of Eric ever since I met her and was talking about him from college. She asked me one day why I didn't marry him, and I told her I was too young to think about marrying anybody at that time, and he and I went our separate ways. Of course, in hindsight, I really should have, and maybe my whole life situation would've turned out differently.

"Then after our date, I did something I know you'd be proud of," I continued. "Him and I went back to the hotel, and let's just say, Trish was right in the blowing-the-back-out part," I chuckled as soon as I said it.

"I knew it. I knew you couldn't resist him, just a little bit," Natalie laughed.

"Yeah, your girl was dry as the Sahara Desert, and I enjoyed every moment of it."

"Toni, you needed this, and you deserved it. Hell, it was the least thing you did after all you've been through. Bad marriage, bad sex, and bad attitude."

"Nooooo," Natalie was going on and on, and I was here for it.

"At least Christian could've had good sex, dang," she continued.

"No, that would've made it that much harder to leave the bastard," I said candidly.

"So are you guys meeting up tomorrow?" she asked.

"Yes, we are, girl. We have a dinner date this time. You know I'm looking forward to the after-dinner dessert," I chuckled, just barely getting that out.

"I heard that, girl. Make sure you have fun for me," Nat said, and we both said our goodbyes and hung up the phone.

I turned on the television and started channel surfing to see what was on. Then my phone rang again. Aye, I must be the woman of the hour, I thought. This time it was Trish. Oh, this should be good—some more questions, I thought.

"Hey, sis, what's up with you?" I asked.

"Girl, not what's up with me. What's up with you? Tell me what happened," she almost demanded.

"Okay, we had a nice date, and he confessed he wanted to rekindle things with me," I continued. "I told him I'd like that, and we're taking it slow, sis," I told her.

"Good, that's good news, Toni."

She genuinely wanted nothing but the best for me in this situation.

"Then we went to the hotel, and you were right."

She laughed loudly.

"I knew that. That man is the true definition of putting in work on your body," she continued. "Seriously, you do know that you needed this, and I wish you much success in this future relationship."

She said, and we continued small talk for several more minutes before ending the call. Trish was always that one sister you could tell your inner thoughts to. She didn't judge—she only listened. She'd always been that way, even when we were younger. She was like a human vault. If you told her something and told her not to repeat it, she did just that. At one point, Dee and I were at odds with each other, and Trish refused to get in the middle of it. Dee and I had to come together on our own.

Dee didn't like Christian and told him to his face she didn't want me to marry him. She thought I deserved so much better. I'd just started dating Christian, and I thought she was making a big deal out of nothing. But what I didn't know was that she saw Christian for who he was—a manipulator. She was on the outside looking in, and even dating him, he had to have things his way. I was young and skipped over all the red flags because I wanted it to work. Dee and I ended up arguing one night about him, and we stopped speaking prior to my wedding date. She didn't show up to the wedding, and neither did her family. She knew I was making a mistake. Years later, she told me she had a bad feeling about him and just couldn't support it when she knew it was wrong. We eventually forgave each other and moved on to have a decent relationship.

Then came the isolation of my family from Christian. I couldn't see it until it was too late. By then, Natalie and Sandra were my only friends. Natalie and I met at the hospital after having one of the many physical beatings courtesy of Christian. At the time, she was an RN in the emergency room. She had a long talk with me about the bruises on my arms and suggested I go to a woman's shelter and press charges on him. It wasn't the first time she'd seen me come through there, and at that moment, she decided to say something.

"The next time—and there will be a next time—you may come in here worse than this or an inch from death," she said with a mix of anger and empathy in her voice.

I was shaking so badly I couldn't even register in my head what she was saying.

"Are you listening and really hearing me?" she said, this time her voice tone becoming concerning.

"Yes, I hear you. I'm scared. He's a lawyer, and he knows the law around this type of thing. He'll just get away with it and get out on bond, and it'll be worse for me," I said through a shaking voice.

"I understand, but you have to wake up and realize it will only be worse for you," she said and proceeded to patch me up.

From that day on, we became good friends, and she slowly helped me start the process of leaving him. She also told him when she'd gotten him alone that she knew what was happening and she had to report it to the authorities. Him, in complete denial, said we had stairs in the house and I'd been drinking and fell down them. She called bullshit and stood by her statement. He said, "You can call them and do what you have to do." Of course, at that time, nothing happened. He talked his way out of it and blamed me for falling. He ended up representing a few of the police officers for half of his fee in exchange for not having to go through the legal process involving "my accident." Natalie made sure to get me to a self-defense class and gave me the name of a good therapist who helped me realize how much my self-esteem had suffered.

"At least you'll have a chance to fight back. Not saying it's right, but he won't be as quick to want to hit you if you pull a few moves on him. At least I hope he won't," she said one night when we were meeting for the self-defense class. "This is until you can save enough money to move the heck out of there."

Slowly, Sandra began to notice too since I'd stopped coming over to her house. When we first moved into the neighborhood, she was one of the first people to come over and welcome us to the area. We instantly clicked and talked over the phone almost daily. She was by herself in what she would call a downgrade home after she'd divorced her husband some years prior. I'd tell her I wanted to start my own real estate business. At the time, I was working as a realtor at one of the local firms but wanted to do it on my own. I'd often put on a brave face in spite of the problems Christian and I started having about four years into our marriage. She'd come over from time to time but never when Christian was home. She told me one time in confidence that she didn't like him. She was polite to him, and he was the same to her. He was always polite to the outsiders but to the people he knew, he was rude and disrespectful. I was at the time making excuses that his personality wasn't for everybody.

As time went on, I realized that was the mask he wanted people to see. He didn't care to create deep bonds with anyone. He had no best friends growing up or in his adult age. She then noticed I'd stopped coming over to her house less, and when she tried to come over to my home and thought Christian wasn't home, he would answer the door. He often told her I wasn't home, even though I was. I had to get a second phone he didn't know about in order to even keep in contact with her and Nat. He tried that with Natalie one time, and she burst past him and called out for me. Nat was a strong personality and an even stronger person—she wasn't hearing it about me not being at home. She knew I hadn't shown up for work in days, and that was alarming. She went upstairs to the bedroom where I was still in bed, reeling from the pain I was in.

Christian had gotten to the point where he didn't take me to the hospital and didn't want me to take myself. He made sure to take my phone where I couldn't even dial 911. There I sat in bed, and Natalie looked at me in horror. Natalie grabbed me and helped me walk down the stairs and told him she had to take me to the hospital. I glanced in the mirror when I got to the bottom of the stairs and didn't recognize the person looking back at me. My right eye was black and blue, and my legs had bruises on them. I had my cream nightgown on, but it had blood on it. Natalie packed me into her car, and we went to the hospital. She'd wrapped me in one of her blankets. I was so out of it I didn't half remember what happened after that. All I knew was one of the doctors said he didn't care what kind of power my husband had and that he'd testify if this case went to court.

This time, the hospital called the police captain and made sure Christian was served with a fine and court appearance. Christian ended up getting a lawyer and paid the charges and pleaded with the judge not to put his law license in jeopardy. He was given a mandatory anger management class. The judge told him if he saw him again, this time he'd lose his law license plus jail time. That was a slight relief I needed because after that, he didn't touch me anymore. We basically avoided each other. I cooked for myself, went about my business taking care of my household duties. He had to wash his own clothes, cook his own food, and could come and go as he pleased.

About a year after that, I got the courage to serve him divorce papers. I filed for separation. He refused and told me he wasn't giving me a divorce. So I told him I wasn't married anymore and gave him back his rings. During this time, Sandra gave me financial advice on how to move most of my money into a private account. It was an investment account that allowed my money to grow. She also told me to redo the divorce paperwork to exclude any commissions from the real estate closings I did. That way, Christian wouldn't be entitled to any of that money.

Natalie and Sandra had seen me at my worst times and at the best times. I couldn't have survived without their friendship. I literally owe my life to them. They came across my path at the right time. I still kept in touch with Sandra and often gave her advice on investing in real estate. She had several properties she rented out, and that was basically her income. I just had to have the right people to give me the strength to finally break away from that damaging situation. So whenever Sandra called, I dropped everything to answer her calls. She often told me how proud she was that I'd divorced him. Those horrible nights I went through, I'd vent to her, and she often asked me to come over to her house—she had more than enough room for me to stay. I refused and told her I didn't want to bring the drama to her doorstep. She often reminded me of Trish and that comforting voice she had. Her and Trish were a few years apart in age from each other, Sandra being older than Trish. When I couldn't talk to my family, I could talk to her.

UNEXPECTED SURPRISES

I cut the television off and went upstairs and slid into the bed. It was later than I thought, and sleepiness had taken over. I slept so well and ended up dreaming about Eric. It was a very good dream indeed. He was in my bed telling me he wanted to spend the rest of his life with me. All I did was turn to him and put my head on his chest and say yes.

The next morning I woke up to the phone ringing. I might have heard it ringing in my dreams—it felt like it.

"Hello," I said into the phone, trying to clear my voice.

It was Dee. This was even early for her.

"Hey, sis, I'm sorry I couldn't sleep last night, and I didn't want to bother you last night," she said. I swear her voice sounded shaky.

"What's wrong, love?" I said.

"Yesterday, Tim served me with divorce papers."

I was taken aback.

"Dee, I am so sorry to hear that."

In all honesty, I thought they were working through their issues. Tim nor Dee seemed like the type to give up when things got tough.

"Me too, and we still haven't told the kids, and I know they're going to be devastated."

You could hear her voice tremble as she tried to stop from crying.

"Listen, if you need to come out again, or the kids, just let me know," I offered.

It was the least I could do given the situation.

"Yeah, I'm just in shock because he told me that he wanted to get past this and work it out. He said, 'I want to be present in my kids' lives.' Now it seems as if he did a 180 and decided that us being separate was for the best."

"Wow," was all I could say in response.

I let Dee vent some more because I knew this news was heavy to bear and hear. I told her I loved her and that if she needed anything, just let me know. I got up and took a shower and got dressed. I had on grey sweatpants and a tan T-shirt. I decided it was a good day to go back to the park to walk. The recent news meant I definitely needed to clear my mind. I'd cook breakfast when I came back. I got to the park in a short amount of time and started my music and put the earbuds in my ears.

I was almost finished with my walk when I received a text from Eric. "Hey, beautiful, I wanted to know what time you'd like to meet for dinner?" I responded back that between six-thirty or seven was fine. "Okay, I'll see you then." He sent the address to the restaurant we were to meet up at. I glanced at the address, and the place looked familiar—I'd only been there once. I was slightly impressed he chose that place. I think I'd had a great workout, so I walked back to the car.

As I drove toward the house, I was quite hungry and couldn't wait to get home to make something to eat. I got in the door and started on some eggs with toast and put some bacon in the oven. The food was done, and I sat down to eat. I heard the phone chiming again. It was Mom this time.

"Hey, Mom, how are you and Dad?"

"Uh-huh, well, that makes sense."

"Okay, I'll do my best to check in on her."

"Love you too."

Hanging up the phone, I thought, well, that was indeed an interesting conversation. I didn't know how Mom did it. How was she so convincing? Mom suggested I have Dee come and stay with me until she saved up enough money to move into her own place. That would mean Dee would have to find a job here, and what if she didn't even like this area? I decided to give her a call and see where her head was at.

"Hey, sis, how are you holding up? Listen, our mom suggested that you come out to visit me and work on relocating here? I know it's a long way from your friends and everyone, but just give it some thought, okay?"

Well, that went well, I thought. Dee sarcastically asked how that was going to work with the upcoming divorce and with the custody agreement Tim conveniently put into place. Tim had gone to the courthouse and requested full custody of their kids. I wasn't shocked by this move. He wanted to use Dee's infidelity as the basis for her being an unfit mother in his eyes. If infidelity was the basis for unfit mothers, then there'd be a lot of mothers losing custody. Dee then stated she had no desire to relocate to the area I was in. She didn't care how much money they were offering. She was approached by more than a few firms in that area, and they all loved her track record and wanted to offer a substantial bonus to join their firm. She declined all of them.

She told me she just couldn't afford to uproot her kids from their routine. In her mind, they needed that stability, especially at the ages they were at. It also didn't make it easier that both she and Tim were lawyers—granted, not in the field of family law—but still, I could see the competition of trying to outdo each other from a mile away. I still secretly thanked God I didn't have a child with Christian. Him being a lawyer, it was ugly, and I could only imagine adding a child into the mix. He had a friend of his whose expertise was family law, too, but he wasn't Christian. Christian was so used to having things his way in criminal law that family law was really foreign to him. Thinking back to the few meetings we had, he had to be talked down a few times by his lawyer. I didn't know how their friendship survived.

I knew she'd be hard to convince—she only dealt with facts and pros versus cons of moving. The fact was she was never going to go for it. I did try. I decided to call up Nat—maybe she had some insight to this situation.

"Hey, Nat, I really need to talk to you."

"Yes, please come over. I think I can explain it better in person."

"Okay, see you in a few."

Hanging up the phone, I looked around and started straightening up the place a bit. I washed the dishes and made sure the kitchen was in a decent state. That was just how I was raised. Couldn't have company coming over to your place when it was, as Mother would say, unkept. Hearing the doorbell ring, I walked toward the door and saw Nat standing there.

"Hey, Nat, come on in," I said.

Natalie had a pair of jean short shorts and a yellow sleeveless shirt, of course with matching yellow wedges. Already standing at five-eight, the wedges made her nearly six feet in height. She had a long flower tattoo on her right thigh.

"Okay, I see someone is enjoying their day off," I noted jokingly.

"Yes, and I intend to take full advantage of the day. So what do you want to discuss?" She got right to the point.

"Mom thought it would be a good idea for Dee to move in with me," I continued. "Dee, of course, gave me every valid reason why she wouldn't do that. Tim also filed for full custody of the children, and to make matters worse, Dee has a certain time to move out of the home they share."

"Oh, wow, this took a very interesting turn," Nat said. "I thought they were trying to work it out in therapy."

"I thought so too, but apparently he'd already made his decision and didn't tell Dee about it until after one of the therapy sessions they had. She told me she won't uproot her kids and that they needed stability at this time."

"Well, I can't blame her there," Nat replied. "I know she, at the end of the day, will do what's best for the kids. I just wish Tim hadn't gone that extreme route on the custody issue," I agreed.

"Right, because in her mind, she's probably shocked he'd call her role as a mother into question. I know I would," Nat said in a serious tone. "It really sounds like he's just trying to get under her skin and make her second-guess her decisions."

"Right. I get that, but why go that route? He knows what type of mom she is and that she'll do anything for her kids," I questioned.

"Well, you know what they say—all is fair in love and war," Nat concluded.

"You want something to drink or eat? I just finished eating breakfast, but I can whip you up something real quick," I asked.

"Okay, I'll take something then. I didn't really eat much before I came over here."

I motioned for her to follow me into the kitchen.

"So what news do you have going on, Nat?" I asked.

I had to change the subject. What my sister was going through was depressing. I never wanted any of my sisters to go through what I went through.

"Girl, me and this guy I met on Tinder went out last night. He thankfully looked like his profile," her voice perked up with excitement. "He was such a gentleman too," she turned around to face me in the chair.

"I'm glad. Just take this slow for me," I said.

"Yes, I will. Besides, he told me he wants to take it slow as well."

"Hmm," I said. "That's always a good sign," I replied, genuinely happy for her.

"I know, and we both have kids, so there's that. We both agreed to start out as friends and then eventually have our kids meet when or if things get serious."

Natalie was at this point grinning from ear to ear.

"Oh my, that smile on your face says it all," I said.

"We talked at the restaurant for what seemed like hours," she confessed. "We have a lot in common. He works in the medical field also, but as a physical therapist," she continued. "He has two kids from a previous marriage."

"Does he want more kids?" I asked.

"Yes, he does, and I think I'd have at least one more," Natalie said.

"Okay, now this does sound promising."

I told her it was about time for her to be happy for once. Natalie and her son had gone through their share of heartbreak. First from her long-term boyfriend, Justin, and then from the few men she'd introduced her son to. Alex was her son. Justin and she met when they were just out of high school. She told me he asked her to marry him a few times, and she'd turn him down. She, in her heart, wasn't ready to get married at that time. Much later into the relationship, they just stayed together and never brought up marriage again. Natalie had her own share of abandonment issues from when her father left her mother. Natalie eventually went to therapy, but that was after Justin decided to leave her. He remained in his son's life and tried to maintain a friendship with Natalie.

In discovering she had abandonment issues, she worked to start healing herself from that trauma. Her and Alex often went to therapy together, and it made a huge difference in their relationship and her relationships with future men. She introduced me to the therapist while I was separating from Christian. It helped me heal from the trauma Christian had put me through. We spent some more time talking, but before we both realized it, it was getting late into the afternoon.

"Hey, what time is your date this evening?" Nat asked.

"In about two more hours. So I appreciate you stopping by and just being a listening ear," I said.

"Do you have your outfit picked out?" she asked.

"Yeah, I think I know what I'm going to wear," I said.

We both got up from the kitchen table and walked toward the front door. We both hugged each other, and Natalie walked outside to her car. Shutting the door behind me, I heard my phone chime. I looked and had received a text from Eric. He sent the address to the restaurant we were meeting at this time. It was on the other side of town this time, so I had to get dressed and beat the traffic madness on a Sunday. I decided this time to wear a nice purple cocktail dress with spaghetti straps. I decided to pair the dress with nice toe-out heels. Besides, it wasn't as hot as yesterday, and this would be more appropriate for the restaurant I was meeting him at.

I glanced around the living room and determined I had everything, so I walked to the door and headed toward the car. Once in the car and out of my neighborhood, I could see the traffic was on the heavy side. I was glad I left early. As I pulled up to the restaurant, it was definitely an elegant pick. The place was located inside of a glass building, which made it seem upscale. I'd admit I hadn't been to this place but heard nothing but good things from the people who'd eaten here. If I liked the food, I thought this could be Nat's and my next eatery to try.

I walked in, and I saw him waiting at the bar, and it seemed like he had a drink in his hand. I motioned to the host that I saw whom I came here for. He nodded and gently walked me over to a table, and Eric walked slowly to where I was seated.

"Hello, beautiful," he said as his eyes were running up and down my body.

"Hello, love," I said while taking in what he had on with my eyes.

I never knew he could wear the hell out of a suit. It fit him very well, and I could tell it was tailored. Of course, he smelled good as well, which didn't help my mind from wandering.

"How was your morning?" I asked.

"It was good. I got to see some of the city, and I really like it here except for the heat," he laughed and continued, "I like the museums and how everyone just loves their city and embraces it."

"Yeah, that's what I fell in love with myself," I interrupted.

"Seriously, though, I could see myself moving to this area," he said.

His voice sounded soothing with a slight twist of Barry White.

"Hmm, are you ready for that type of move?"

"Friends that truly love you will be with you wherever you decide to go," I said.

"Well, were you looking to possibly move anywhere else?" he asked innocently.

"I'm open to that possibility. I've thought about it a few times but have no real clue of where that would be," I said, looking at him and felt the urge to reach across the table and hold his hand.

I did just that. I had to be honest with him and tell him about what I needed from a relationship.

"I know we're taking this slow. I just want to say that I've worked past the trauma of my past marriage, and I'm ready to move to something better. I know you have your kids that you're raising, but I need to be a priority along with the kids. I need you to know that I cannot be secondary to your work either. In my past relationships and marriage, I was always pouring into other people and never had that in return. I need this if we're going to work toward having a relationship."

He looked at me and in a serious tone said,

"I know, Toni, and I will always make you a priority. I have shared custody with my kids, and their mother and I are on friendly terms. So you don't have to worry about that part. I have every intention of making you a part of both my kids' and my life."

Hearing that made me feel at peace within.

"Anything you want to do other than real estate, I'll support you 100 percent. I know how special and talented you are."

I just stared at him and said to myself, where have you been all my life? I almost had tears in my eyes because I'd never heard anyone say that to me. It made my heart melt. Right on cue, the waiter came over to take our orders. I felt that what he said was heartfelt. After taking our orders, the waiter walked back to the computer to put the orders in.

"I'm serious, Toni. I didn't think we'd ever cross paths again, and I told myself that if we did and you were no longer married, I'd make you mine."

"Wow, I don't know what to say," I confessed.

"I had come across your sister's phone number from searching for something else, and I didn't know if she still had the same number, but I dialed it anyway. We talked for a long time, and when she told me you were divorced, I couldn't help but be excited," he said. "I want to be a part of your life, Toni, if you let me."

By this time, he had a glimmer in his eyes and a slight smile on his face.

"Yes, I'd like that," I nodded, thinking this was a second chance at love and someone who would love me in the way I should be loved.

After what seemed like hours eating and drinking at the restaurant, we proceeded to leave and head toward the hotel. I felt excited, hopeful, and anxious all at the same time. When we arrived at the hotel, both of us were feeling the effects of the alcohol. We moved over to the bed, and I started undressing him first this time, and I turned around so he could slip me out of my dress. There we stood, both grinning and naked. I pushed him onto the bed and decided to get on top this time. As I pushed him in me, I felt all of him fill me up. I began to ride him, and my juices were running down, wanting him, inviting him further in. He put his hands on my breasts, gently caressing them, and then reached up and started kissing them, fully putting them into his mouth, sucking on each one at a time. I started going faster, and this feeling, this pleasure—I never wanted it to end.

As I moaned, I felt an escalating pleasure as I climaxed, and it seemed to last forever. Then I heard him moan in response, and he started climaxing as well. I made sure to keep the stride going until I felt his heartbeat slow down. I collapsed on top of him, and he lifted my head up and started to kiss me deeply—one of those soul-searching kisses. I scooted my body to the side of him, and we just held each other until we fell asleep.

The next morning, the sunlight was peeking through a slit in the curtains, and I woke up to him kissing me again.

"I really could get used to this," I confessed.

I had a hangover, but nothing coffee couldn't cure.

"Good morning, sexy," I said after our lips departed.

"Good morning, beautiful. I have a flight in a few hours, so I'm going to jump into the shower. I left my card out on the table. Feel free to order breakfast."

I got up and went over to look at the hotel menu and ordered him and me bacon, eggs, and toast with orange juice. I clicked on the television to catch up on the morning news. I walked over to the bathroom door and peered in.

"Do you mind if I join you?" I asked.

"Come on in. The water is nice and steamy," he motioned me to come toward him.

I gathered my hair up into a ponytail and slid the shower door back and hopped in. The water was beaming off of his body, and we switched places so I could get some of it. It was nice, hot, and steamy. He'd pretty much already washed himself off, so he grabbed the washcloth and filled it with soap to wash me off. His hands felt so good scrubbing my body down. I turned to face him so he could get in front of me as well. I felt so tingly inside as his hands glided from one body part to the other. After thoroughly washing me down, I rinsed off the excess soap. He opened the shower door and stepped out, drying off and started brushing his teeth and getting dressed.

I was in my head, thinking of last night and what spending the rest of my life would be like with him. Also thinking, am I ready to take on the role of being a stepmother? I was getting too far ahead of myself, I thought. I jumped out of the shower and wiped off my face and dried off my body. I grabbed some perfume to put on and slid into a white pair of jean shorts with a teal tank top. He'd dressed in brown khaki shorts and a dark green polo shirt.

"I see you're ready for the flight, huh?" I looked at him

and felt the urge to give him a kiss.

As we kissed, room service knocked at the door. He walked to the door and opened it so the staff could come in. Everything looked good on the table, even how they fancy tied the napkins. We sat down and ate and realized the time just jumped away from us.

"I'm getting out of here, and I'll call you once I'm back in Cali," he said as he started walking to the door with his luggage in hand.

"Okay, have a safe flight."

Then the door shut. I gathered up the rest of the clothes, put them in my overnight bag, and went to the door. Looking down into my purse, I spotted the keys. Opening the door, I looked back in the room one last time, remembering the wonderful night we'd had. I walked to the car, and my cell phone started ringing as soon as I got into the car.

"Good morning, Trish," I giggled.

That lady's timing never ceased to amaze me. She asked how day two was with mister.

"It was great, and it's like we never were apart, honestly."

I told her what he said to me at dinner. She told me she had a feeling he wanted to reconnect on a deeper level than just a one-night stand.

"I'm on my way back to the house after I stop and run some errands. Love you too, and talk to you later."

I hung up the phone. I had to stop by the store to get a few items I wanted to make for dinner. After coming out of the store, I put the items in the car and walked next door to the dry cleaners. I picked up two suits and a pair of dress pants. I got into the car and headed toward the house. I grabbed the items and walked into the door. I sat the groceries on the counter and put the clothes on the sofa. My cell rang again. This time it was Kevin. I was kind of shocked he'd reach out to me because he'd usually call when the shit had hit the fan, so to speak.

"Hey, lil bro, what's going on?" I asked as I put away the things I'd brought from the store.

He started telling me about the conversation Dee and he had about her coming to live with him. He offered to find her a place and put in a good word with a few of the lawyers he knew to see if she could come aboard with their prospective law firms.

"Let me guess, she didn't want to hear it?" I nodded when he told me yes.

She didn't even listen to him get the conversation out before she shut him down.

"I told her the kids will adjust to having to move to a new city if there are better opportunities than staying at the firm she's at while having to work around Tim."

I didn't see a way around having to come across him every month for their meetings and it not feeling awkward. Kevin said he'd even already talked to a lawyer friend of his with his own law firm who very much wanted Dee to come and work with him. His firm had all sorts of specialties in law, but he didn't have a corporate lawyer. Dee's reputation was a big deal in the corporate law arena. She acted modest on her accomplishments, but she'd been featured several times on the cover of a few law magazines. She had a list of clients who raved about her service and loyalty to them. She usually named her price and had no problem getting it. I just found it hard to believe she'd want to keep her kids and herself in a situation she didn't have to be in.

"Kevin, I tried to reason with her, and basically she's going to do what she wants. I don't want her to stay at the cost of her mental health. No one is looking out for her, but you can't get her to see that."

Kevin talked for several minutes longer and said he was done trying. I totally understood that feeling. He had to go back and tell his lawyer friend she decided to stay where she was. Kevin even told Dee what the friend was willing to offer to compensate for her move to that area and her relocation expenses fully paid for.

"Well, bro, I love you, and take care of yourself. Don't worry, I'm sure Dee will come around."

I hung up the phone. Boy, this had been a busy day, I thought to myself. My sister was set on being miserable just to prove to Tim he didn't get under her skin. The kids even saw they were miserable around each other. I decided to start looking at my calendar for the new year appointments while I was attempting to clean up the house. I went upstairs to my office and started gathering potential homes for the clients. I gathered the first four clients who had appointments in the first two weeks after the new year. I went online and pulled three to four houses apiece. Some were in their price range, and some were outside of their price range but were negotiable.

Then I heard the doorbell ring. Slightly startled, I made my way down the stairs to see who it was. No one just showed up unannounced, and I damn sure hoped it wasn't my ex-husband. I wouldn't put that past him. When I opened the door, to my surprise, it was a FedEx delivery. The rep asked me to sign for the package. As soon as I did, there was a gigantic bouquet of yellow roses. I took the flowers and put them on the table. I turned around and shut the door. Still in shock, the roses were so beautiful and different.

"Wow," was all I said out loud.

Then I saw the card and decided to open it. "I am so glad to have you back in my life. I want you to feel this special every day. Signed, Eric." My heart swelled and melted at the same time. I was still gasping at the amount of flowers in this vase. The vase itself was massive, standing at least three feet tall and crystal with designs etched into the glass. Then there were at least three dozen roses in this vase. It was so breathtaking. I knew Eric was still in the air, so I sent him a simple thank-you text.

My cellphone started chiming, and I looked down, and it was Natalie.

"Hey, Nat, how are you doing?"

"Oh, were you responsible for these flowers? They're so beautiful, and I see he consulted with you. Always my girl looking out for me. Okay, no, at the moment I'm just getting some clients and homes together for next week. Okay, see you when you get here."

I hung up the phone. Natalie was responsible for Eric sending me the flowers. He asked her what type of flowers I liked and the color. I swear she had my back, even in the shadows.

NEW YEARS SPARKS

I was actually looking forward to her coming over. I thought I wanted to go out for New Year's Eve. While she was en route, I went upstairs to see what I could wear for tonight. Not even sure if we were just going to one bar or bar hopping. Definitely had to make sure I had some comfortable heels on. Secretly, I wanted to do a bit of flirting. Besides, Eric and I hadn't taken what we had to the next level yet.

Looking in the closet, I didn't know if I wanted to dress over the top or chic and simple. I pulled out a few options. The first dress was short and sparkled all over. It was silver with a deep V-neck. That would be good for putting the twins on display. Option two was a red long sleeveless dress with a slit going to the upper thigh. My arms were decently toned to pull this dress off, except I wasn't in the mood for wearing a long dress. Short dresses showed my legs, which I liked better than my arms. They also accentuated my backside better. Option three was a short dress in a deep purple color that had wide straps but was lacy. My semi-romantic dress. I had the perfect purple heels to go with it too. I decided to wear the purple dress.

"Ringggg." Interrupted by the doorbell, I went downstairs to greet Nat.

"Hey, come on in," I motioned for her to walk with me upstairs.

"Girl, I am so ready to go out somewhere tonight," she confessed. "I think if we bar hop, we may as well take a Lyft to get there."

Nat glanced at the three dresses on the bed. I pulled out the shoes I thought would look best with them.

"You know I love that purple one, and you seem to get a lot of attention with it too," she looked down and saw the purple shoes. "Now these are comfortable to walk in, right?" She laughed.

"Yes, they are, despite how they look. The heel isn't that high to me."

I then put the rest of the dresses and shoes away.

"So we bar hopping or going to one good bar?" I asked.

"Girl, the most we'll do is three bars. I don't have it in me to do more than that, and I have to go to work tomorrow.

I frowned up my face.

"Man, that's why I don't like the medical field. No actual days off unless you take them."

"Yeah, you know it," she said, then grabbed one of the bags from the closet and put my shoes and clothes in it. "We can leave from my house since the bars are closer to where I live."

I agreed. I added some change of clothes to the bag as well as a toothbrush, toothpaste, shower essentials, and sneakers. It was a good idea that we were going there and not having to worry about finding parking, paying crazy fees for said parking, and getting into the bar. We grabbed everything and walked back down the stairs. Nat stared hard at the flowers this time.

"You did good, Nat. When did he have time to order these?" I asked.

"He had a slight flight delay and called me and asked what he could get you for having a great time this weekend. I told him flowers always work for you."

I nodded and said, "You're not lying, and he outdid himself. How is your sister Dee doing?"

"We got to get into that conversation at your house. It's too much to tell you here. We'll be running late if I tell you now."

Natalie and I walked out the door. I made sure to lock up and put the alarm on. She jumped into her car, and I followed her to her home. As soon as we arrived at her house, I started telling her the conversation I had with Kevin about Dee. Nat was taken aback.

"If she wants to stay in the same state, why can't she join another firm?"

I shook my head.

"I don't know, but it would seem easier than staying in a potential toxic work environment," I said.

Natalie's home was sunny and bright like her personality. Her walls, specifically in the living room, were pale blue with orange furniture. She always liked contemporary pieces.

Glass and silver everywhere. She had several pieces of art hanging on the walls. The kitchen was white and gold with gold fixtures. It still amazed me how she kept it so spotless with a child in the house, especially with the amount of glass tables she had. The hallway was a deep cream color with various paintings hanging throughout. She'd said a long time ago she wouldn't want a two-story house. So the bedrooms were on one side of the house, and the living room, dining area, and kitchen were on the other side. Her bedroom was a deep burgundy color. She had a mirror-style dresser and nightstands. The bed itself had a low headboard and wrought iron. She walked over to the closet and began looking for clothes.

"Okay, I think since you're wearing a short dress, I want to choose one similar to the one you picked," she then glanced at the bottom of the closet at the shoe selection. "I think I want to put on the red stilettos and hopefully my feet won't betray me."

"Well, I think your feet will be okay as long as you don't start to feel too good from the alcohol," I chimed in and immediately laughed.

"Yeah, good one, Toni," Nat chuckled in response. "I think this dress would be perfect."

She pulled out a red strapless with a mermaid-like shape and at the bottom two rows of lace. The dress was definitely a showstopper, and I didn't think I'd ever seen her wear this one.

"I just ordered this one about two weeks ago."

"Ahh, okay, I knew I hadn't seen this one before."

I knew exactly where Nat's money went—shoes and clothes. We started getting ready by Nat pouring us a few drinks. I was more of a dark liquor girl, and Nat was more of a light liquor. I did every now and then like a good margarita. We then started getting dressed, and Nat put the request in for the Uber driver to pick us up. Both of us felt good and sexy as we headed out for the evening events.

The first bar we stopped at was crowded, but the atmosphere was that of peace and good vibes. The conversations were lively. Nat and I decided to sit at the bar and have a few shots. It wasn't long before two gentlemen walked over—both were handsome from the angle I could see, one white and another one Black.

"How are you ladies doing tonight?" the white guy politely asked us.

"We're doing great," I said, and then I really noticed both of them.

They were dressed in nice suits, not black tie but darn close. I'd by that time turned my chair around for an even better look. Both of them were tall and both were here on vacation, on leave from the military.

"So I know you two have drinks, but would you like to dance with us?" he asked. "Oh, I'm being rude. I'm Kurt, and my friend here is Rob," he said as they both exchanged handshakes with us.

"Hi, this is Natalie, and I'm Toni," I said back, wanting to at least dance with one of them.

Natalie wanted to kick herself for the shoes she had picked. I noticed Kurt was feeling a sister. He'd lean in when I'd talk and make piercing eye contact. He and Rob were definitely easy on the eyes. I glanced around the room at the other men and women in here, and I'd say, based on the amount of people, they might have asked one other set of women to dance. I felt comfortable with those odds. They weren't the only good-looking ones here, which was a good thing.

"Okay, let's hit that dance floor," I got up, and he grabbed my hand and led the way.

As I walked, I turned around and saw Natalie still talking to Rob.

"So what do you do? Do you live in the area?" He started asking a lot of questions.

"I do live in the area, and I'm in the real estate business. I own my own real estate company."

"Oh, that sounds good. I came out here with my friend for vacation since we're stationed in San Antonio."

I nodded and asked, "So you didn't want to go out to Galveston where the beach is? The city is considered a vacation spot for you?"

"No, we already went to Galveston, and it's okay but just not for us."

We were dancing to some jams from the early 2000s, and I was in a zone. The DJ was spinning nothing but hits. I glanced over to my left, and Natalie was on the dance floor with Rob. They seemed to be really hitting it off.

"I'm going back to the bar and resting for a minute," I walked away, and he, of course, followed behind me.

"I know the night is winding down, but I'd like to get to know more about you, Toni," he said.

I thought to myself it was interesting because I really didn't think I was his type. Then again, maybe he didn't have one.

"Okay, give me your phone so I can add my number to it."

As he handed me his phone, I put my number in and called it from my phone.

"This is me," I said.

"I know I'm not in the area for long, but I can always come and visit you."

Was this dude already falling in love? I thought to myself.

"I'm open to that," I said, and the DJ started announcing it was time for the countdown for the new year.

I stood up, and we watched the countdown show on the main big screen in front of us. The DJ began the countdown.

"10... 9... 8... 7... 6... 5...," the DJ announced, and the staff started passing around champagne to toast to.

Kurt grabbed two for both of us.

"4... 3... 2... 1... HAPPY NEW YEAR."

We both toasted, and unbeknownst to me, Kurt reached in for a kiss. I was taken aback by surprise. The kiss was sensual and calming, not rushed or forced. He put his arms around me as we kept kissing through the New Year song. His tongue and my tongue interlocked in each other's mouths. His tongue knew the right stroke so my tongue would feel so comfortable. This guy had a master's degree in kissing. I think we kissed for what seemed like an eternity.

"Em humm," I heard someone clearing their throat.

I looked, and both of us unlocked our kisses. It was Natalie. Rob was standing behind her with a grin on his face. I looked at Kurt, and he smiled, and I gushed like a schoolgirl just being caught kissing in the bathroom. By this time, the lights were starting to come on fully, and we both got a good look, and thankfully it wasn't the lighting that was making these two look good. Kurt was tall and skinny with a brown low haircut. His face was wonderfully chiseled, which made it seem like he was a model rather than in the military. Rob was muscular and also had a low haircut, no facial hair except for a mustache and big eyes. His physique was definitely Nat's type. She loved them muscular and physically intimidating. He might be too clean-cut for her, though.

"Hey, we'll be back. We're going to the restroom," she mentioned and motioned for me to follow her.

"Girl, I didn't mean to interrupt, but I really had to pee, and I didn't want to walk by myself to the bathroom," she confessed. "I really like Rob, though, and wish he was here longer than just a few days."

"Why?" I asked.

"My schedule is crazy, and I told him what I did, but he still wanted to see me and said he'd make the time."

"Well, that sounds good and promising. Nat, please don't start self-sabotaging before you get to know the guy. He seems like a real gentleman."

"I know, I know, and I'm not. I'm trying to keep an open mind."

She ran into the stall to do her business. I started looking at myself in the mirror, and my phone chimed. It was Kurt asking if we were okay and if we needed a ride home. I texted him back to wait for us and we wouldn't be much longer. Natalie came out of the stall and washed her hands.

"Do you want them to take us home?" I asked her.

"Yeah, let's get them to drive us to my house," she said. "I'll take you home in the morning."

That was the best idea because half of Nat's family was law enforcement, and they didn't play when it came to her safety. She literally had a cousin who was a detective residing in the next street over. She always texted him when she and I went out and when she went out on dates so that if anything went left, he knew where to come look for her.

"Okay, let's go," I said as we left the bathroom and walked toward both of the men.

"We're back, and yes, you two can take us to Natalie's house."

"Okay, let's go," Kurt motioned us toward the door, and once outside, the chill in the air hit us in the face.

We followed Kurt and Rob to a black BMW truck. Kurt said, "Here we are, ladies," and proceeded to get into the driver's side. Nice taste, I thought to myself. I also thought to myself, this was a pimp truck if I ever saw one. An immediate panty dropper, I chuckled out loud.

"What are you over there laughing about?" Kurt asked as we were driving toward Nat's home.

"Oh, nothing," I said and continued to look around at the sights as a passenger.

I always saw things I never saw while I was driving. I was also trying to hear Nat's conversation with Rob and how that was going. I got a good feeling about those two. Natalie had a strong personality, and most men said she was too opinionated, but this one didn't seem shy about being around her. I hoped this one was true love for her, even with her flaws. He seemed to have a good head on his shoulders and goals for himself.

"We're about ten minutes out until we reach Natalie's home," Kurt said. "I really enjoyed my time with you, Toni."

"I enjoyed my time with you as well, Kurt."

"I hope to see you again next week if your schedule permits," he added. "You make a person feel comfortable to be around you, and I don't know when the last time was that

I've felt like that," he confessed.

I really didn't know what to say at this point. I knew Eric wanted to be serious about me, but he was still long distance, and not knowing how travel, who came to see who, would work out. Now Kurt was confessing he wanted to keep seeing me. I had a lot to think about at this point.

"I'd like to see you again," I agreed because he was here at this moment. He might not want to get serious yet.

"We're here," he announced, and all of us got out of the truck and walked toward Nat's house.

Kurt and I stayed behind a bit and talked some more. He asked if I could see him next weekend, and I told him I could do that. Natalie and Rob were at the doorstep talking, and he told her she had a nice home. She said thanks and opened the door, and before I knew it, they were kissing at the door. She told him goodbye and walked in, and he started walking down the walkway toward us. As we inched closer to the door, Kurt decided to kiss me again. I felt the same sparks I'd felt at the bar. We looked at each other, and he said goodnight and walked back toward the truck.

"Get to your destination safely, and even if it's late, text me when you get there."

I turned around and walked into the house.

"Girl, I can't wait to tell you what Rob and I were talking about," Natalie was already seated on the sofa, still excited.

I closed the door and said, "I want to hear all about it."

I dropped onto the sofa and started taking off my shoes. Nat's shoes were already off. In fact, I think she took them off in the truck.

"Rob was like, 'What do I have to do to get in your

space? I want to see more of you, and I'm not looking for just a casual date.'"

I was surprised a bit because Rob seemed like the player type. My first impression was that, but maybe I was wrong on that assessment. She continued,

"He said, 'I saw you as soon as you and your homegirl walked into the place. You two definitely stood out, and I was mesmerized when I approached you at the bar.' Kurt had to hype me up a bit because I was scared to really come over, and he said, 'Come on, they both are lookers, and they may be taken or they might not be.'"

Natalie said both of them looked over at us and just knew we weren't single. Rob said both of them almost jumped when they found out we were and didn't want to let the opportunity pass by to exchange information.

"That was about it, but I have to change these clothes and go to bed," she jumped up and went toward the bedroom.

I forgot she had to work later on. I went with her to grab my bag and change my clothes, and then I reached into the hall closet to get one of the blankets. I slumped down onto the sofa and tried to get as comfortable as possible.

THE SERPENT RETURNS

efore I knew it, the sun was peeking through the blinds, and she didn't have blackout curtains in the living room, so the whole room lit up with sunshine. I had a slight headache but didn't feel sick, thankfully. Having a hangover was the worst, and throwing up was no fun to anyone. What a time we'd had last night, though. I heard the coffee machine in the kitchen getting someone's cup ready. I glanced up and saw Natalie walking over toward me.

"Hey, are you feeling okay?"

"I could be better, have a slight headache."

"Okay, I'm going to get you some pain pills and water. I made you some coffee, and I already had mine so I can at least pretend to be functional at work today."

Natalie laughed, and I just shook my head because I agreed that work was the last thing on anyone's mind after last night. Natalie already had on her scrubs for work and walked back in to give me the pain pills and a glass of water.

"I'm going to be in the kitchen whenever you get yourself together."

I nodded and sat up slightly to take in the water to chase the pain pills down. I got up and walked toward the bathroom in the hall with a washcloth and shower gel and started running the water for a quick shower. I just needed to wake up these eyes, and coffee would do the rest. After getting out of the shower and drying off, I wrapped the towel around me to go back into the living room and throw on some comfortable clothes. I put on some gray leggings and a bright green top. I knew I wouldn't be walking in the park today.

"What time do you have to leave, Nat?"

"I don't have to leave until two hours from now, but I wanted to make sure I had everything packed for work and had time to get my mind together. I did get a good morning text from you-know-who."

"Ahhh, starting on a positive note, I see."

"Yeah, he wished me a good day at work and hoped my work shift will go fast."

I walked over to the K-cup machine and grabbed the cup of coffee that was still steaming hot, waiting for me. My phone vibrated on the table, and Nat said,

"Dang, the whole table almost shook from your phone."

I laughed.

"I know that vibration can be right strong."

As I sat down, I grabbed the phone and noticed it was a good morning text from Kurt. Then another one had come in from Eric. I shook my head and realized I had to see what potential there was for Kurt and me if I was wanting to be with Eric. Natalie grabbed her keys, and I grabbed my bag, and we were headed out the door. Nat put in my address on GPS, and we took off.

"I'm going to text Rob back that I want to see him again sometime this week."

"Yesssss, that sounds promising, Nat."

"I know, but I have to let him know if he's serious, then he has to do above the bare minimum. Besides, time is money, right."

I nodded in agreement.

"He has to show how much he's interested in me by his actions. I've had enough dudes in my life to talk the talk but not put action behind it. They start out strong but then start losing interest, and that's where they lose me."

I couldn't agree more with her statement. Men lost interest by their actions, and that was the one thing that turned me off in dating again.

"I hear you, Nat. Let your intentions be known from the beginning, and we shall see where his head is at."

Once we arrived at my house, I gave Nat a hug and told her,

"Take care of yourself today. Try not to work so hard, and let them folks know it's a holiday and I'm only one person."

"I will, Toni. Take a break when you want to because you deserve it."

As I shut the car door, I grabbed my bag out of the back seat and walked toward the house. I turned around and waved at her as she blew the horn as she was driving away. Once in the house, I clicked on the television, putting the bag down by the stairs. I still felt sort of sleepy, but my headache was no longer there. I slid onto the sofa and mindlessly started channel surfing. I then decided to open up one of the streaming apps and started looking for a good movie I could watch and probably fall asleep on. Not long into the movie, I'd fallen asleep, and the phone ringing woke me up. It was Trish.

"Hey, Trish, what's going on?" I was still half asleep.

"No, I was on the sofa taking a nap. Happy New Year to your family. I know, I'm about to send out a New Year text to everyone. I had a great time last night, and I met someone."

"No, Eric and I have not talked about getting into a relationship yet, Trish. We're taking it slow, so until then, we both are still single."

"Yes, he knows that. His name is Kurt, and he seems like a sweet guy. We had a good time dancing and just getting to know one another."

"I know that, and I love you, but come on with the questions, sis. I know you're just looking out for me. I'm not rushing into anything yet."

"Yes, I'm going to talk to Dee once I'm fully awake."

By this time, I knew Trish was sensing that my tone had become elevated. Sometimes she could be so intense, though, that she didn't think about how her inquiry made people feel.

"Okay, I love you too, and tell everyone I said hi."

Hanging up the phone, I stared at the ceiling for five minutes and took some deep breaths. Trish and her older sister tendencies could be a bit much. She literally forgot I was a full-grown adult with a business and a mortgage to pay. I clicked on my list of contacts in my phone and sent out several Happy New Year gifs and memes, especially to the family and friends. My clients—I sent out emails to them. It was more personable than a simple gif text.

I decided to call Dee and see where her headspace was at.

"Happy New Year, Dee."

"You're finalizing the divorce this month. Wow. Okay, and you're still working out the custody arrangements. So he doesn't want you to move out of state because he doesn't feel like having to travel to pick up the kids. Have you thought about moving to another city within that area?"

"Dee, I know you're upset, and rightfully so. You just have to find a compromise somewhere. Have you been talking with the therapist? I mean, I think you should consider medication if that's what the therapist feels is best for you. Okay, I love you. Talk to you later."

Just like that, Dee hung up. Once she had her mind made up, there was only God himself who could talk her out of it. In my heart, I felt like Dee wasn't following through with the therapist like she was telling everyone. I decided to call Trish and figure out what she knew about what was going on.

"Hey, Trish, I just got off the phone with Dee, and I had a strange conversation with her. Do you know what's going on with her? When was the last time you two spoke?"

"I don't know, but her voice doesn't sound right to me. I don't think she's going to the therapist anymore. I say that because when she said the therapist thought she should take medication, Dee ended the session and abruptly left. That means she hasn't been back to the therapist in over a month. I don't think she wants to hear that she has to take medication. Who knows? I think Dee thinks it makes her seem weak."

"I don't know, Trish, but can you reach out to her? I'm telling you, something doesn't feel right. Okay, I love you too. Talk to you later."

Trish thought I was overreacting, but Dee did not sound like herself. She sounded distant, almost like she was spaced out about something. She wasn't present on the phone—she just answered questions I asked, but no feeling or nothing behind it. I'd never seen her like this, and frankly, it was scaring me. I didn't want to call our parents because I didn't want them to worry either. Knowing Dad, he'd immediately book a flight to see her. The situation she was going through wasn't good, and I didn't think she was handling it well at all. Since Trish and Leon were closer to her to drive or fly if they wanted, they could go and check in on her. I thought she might have reached her breaking point. It was what she didn't say that I didn't have a good feeling about. I knew my sister, and something was off about her. I also knew that if anything wasn't sounding good when she talked to Trish, Trish would be on the next flight to her place. We never played about our family. This situation was no different.

I finished up watching the movie on the television and then sent a text to Nat to check in on her. "Hey, just checking in on you. Don't work too hard now, it's the holiday. Call me when you can. I need to talk to you about the conversation Dee and I had. Xoxo." I got up and went into my office. I started checking through my calendar to see what appointments I had this week. I had about three houses to show plus a few listings that were coming up. I went through and made sure each house had an open house event that was still confirmed. Then combed through the emails from a few of the clients who wanted to list their homes. I replied to confirm what month and date they wanted to start the process of listing their homes.

I glanced down at my phone and received a response back from Nat. "Hey, I am hanging in here. As you can imagine, people are idiots on New Year's Day. I've had a few hangovers, some accidents, some dummies thinking they're invincible, and I am beyond ready to go at this point. I'm trying not to work hard, but tell that to the stupid people that keep coming in here messed up. I will call you later. I am promptly leaving in three hours, and that can't come fast enough. LOL. Xoxo." I started shaking my head as soon as I read through her text. I still stood by my agreement that I was so glad I didn't pick the medical field. That and the sight of blood made me squeamish.

I sat at my desk and looked through the homes the clients wanted to list. I asked them to schedule a date and time for me to come by and take a look at each property. I went back down the stairs after about an hour of organizing the listings I had coming up and confirmed all the open house appointments. Hearing my phone chime again, I thought it was Nat, but instead it was my other friend, Sandra.

"Hey, Sandra, how have you been doing?"

"Wait. What do you mean he's coming to see me?"

"Yes, I still have the order of protection in place. I don't understand. I can hardly understand what you're saying."

"Okay, but he's not stupid enough to show up here unless he wants to get himself arrested. Okay, okay, I understand. He came to see you. That is strange."

Hanging up the phone, I felt my anxiety go from one to 100 instantly. Apparently, my ex-husband showed up at Sandra's house, warning her he was going to find me. When I moved to the place I was at now, I made sure to keep an order of protection on file with the local police. What Sandra was saying didn't make sense, I thought to myself. The judge had warned him that if he parked so much as across the street from where I lived, he'd be arrested. So Sandra told me this, and immediately I had to text Nat that I might be in danger. "Hey, Nat, I got some very disturbing news from Sandra. If you call and I don't answer the phone, call the police. Immediately. I think my ex-husband is up to something, and Sandra doesn't know what it is. I know he popped up at her place unexpectedly. He didn't tell her what it was, and she tried to stop him from figuring out where I live. I am scared right now, and I don't know what is about to happen. Xoxo."

I couldn't brush off this feeling I had in the pit of my stomach. I decided to book a hotel stay just in case he did show up at my house. I went upstairs to pack for at least two days. I didn't want to text Eric, and I didn't know Kurt long enough to even begin to tell him about my ex. I knew Eric would literally fly out and sit at the house waiting for Christian to show up. I didn't want that on my conscience. That could lead to assault charges, and I didn't want Eric to go through all of that. This was crazy—why would he risk his career and law license... I stopped mid-thought. Unless he did something after him and I split up with someone else. Oh my God, what if he'd already lost his license because of someone else? Oh, this was not good, I thought to myself.

When he and I split, I cut all communication. I basically had to. Sandra was the only one from that neighborhood I talked with, and even she didn't know where I'd moved to. She only knew I was safe and that I'd had to sell the house he and I shared. Immediately, I got on the phone with the police. I told them I might be in danger but wasn't 100 percent sure. I told them about the conversation my neighbor had with my ex-husband. I also told them he was extremely dangerous and to have someone come over to sit at my house. They, of course, asked how he found me if I had no communication with him.

They asked my name on the mortgage, and I told them it was, and that Christian knew people who could get him that information. All he had to do was pay them the right price.

Again, I thought he went to Sandra's place because he thought she knew where I'd moved to. When she didn't know, he must've paid someone to track me down. This couldn't be real. This couldn't be happening, I thought. The police told me they'd send someone over to sit at my house. Due to the fact that I had an order of protection and the past incidents on file that were sent over to them when I moved, they took me seriously. I told them I'd booked a hotel because I wasn't sure what he'd do if I stayed here. They suggested I cancel the hotel stay and just stay at the house. I didn't agree, but I went along with it.

Almost jumping out of my skin, the doorbell shocked me back into reality. The police on the phone told me to answer the door. Opening the door, the officer greeted me and told me he'd be sitting in the car and pointed toward the direction where the car was. The officer on the phone told me they'd be there all night to make sure I was safe. Meanwhile, the officer at the door introduced himself, and I could see the name on his tag and the ID number on his badge. Hanging up the phone, I felt a little less anxious, but that pit in my stomach still hadn't gone away.

"I'll be in the car. If I see anything suspicious, I'll call it in."

I nodded, and as he walked away, I shut the door. I still didn't feel good and reached out to my parents.

"Hey, Mom, I'm okay, but wanted you to know if anything should happen, remember that I love you and Dad."

"No, don't worry, I'm fine. Mom, no, don't book a flight. I'll be okay. No, I already talked to Trish. I'm good. I talked to Dee also, and if you can reach out to her and make sure she's doing okay. I mean, when I spoke to her, she didn't sound like she was the usual calm and collected self. She sounded like she was a million miles away from here even though she was talking to me on the phone. I don't know what happened, and I really don't think she's been to the therapist lately. Okay, I love you guys, and I'll talk to you later."

Natalie beeped while I was on the phone. I switched over to tell her what was going on with me and with Dee.

"No, you don't have to come over, Nat. The police sent someone to sit outside of my house. Okay, if you insist, then I'll see you when you get here."

Hanging up the phone, I knew Nat wouldn't be getting off from work for another three hours. I knew she sensed the uneasiness in my voice and just wanted to be around to make sure I was okay. I still had a lot of emotions going through my head, and even though the officer was outside, I still had a bad feeling that wouldn't leave me. I tried to look through a few movies on the television until Nat got off from work. That, of course, didn't ease my mind one bit. I went into the kitchen to try and fix something to eat to settle my stomach. I fixed some stir-fry noodles, shrimp, and broccoli. I sat at the table, hoping this would work to calm my nerves down.

I was halfway finished when I thought I heard a popping sound, almost sounding like firecrackers. I looked around and thought, no one does fireworks on New Year's Day. I just shook my head and continued eating the food. Just in case, I went to the living room window and looked out at the police car that was still parked across the street. I didn't see anything wrong or out of place. I shook my head again and walked back into the kitchen and started putting the dishes and pans in the sink. I jumped as I heard what sounded like the door being kicked in, hard. I rushed to the door to see what was happening.

"CHRISTIAN, WHAT ARE YOU DOING HERE?" I screamed.

I glanced to the side of him at the now-broken front door, and as I glanced toward the car again, I could clearly see that a round hole was in the driver's side window. I screamed again because the help I thought I had was no longer there. Christian looked like he'd gained at least forty pounds of muscle and had a look in his eyes I'd never seen before. Almost a dark, blank stare. His eyes were soulless.

"Listen, you don't have to do this. We can talk this out, whatever it is."

He didn't say anything and just grabbed me as hard as he could. I scratched him across his neck in the struggle to get away. I attempted to run into the kitchen to get to the sliding door. He tripped me by grabbing my legs. He then brought out a gun as he was now on top of me in the kitchen.

"How did you even find me?"

My cell phone was still on the kitchen table, and I thought about how I could get to the table while he was still trying to pin me down.

"Don't worry about how I found you. Just know you're the cause of this and what's about to happen," he said. His voice was almost unrecognizable.

I'd never seen this side of him, and I felt my survival instincts kick in. He kept trying to pin me tighter in his grip. I kicked him in the sides with all my force, and he jumped off of me in pain. I leaped over to where my phone was on the table and pressed 911.

"911, what's your emergency?"

Pop.

www.ingramcontent.com/pod-product-compliance
Lightning Source LLC
Chambersburg PA
CBHW060405310726
48976CB00003B/948